PRINCESS BARI

Hwang Sok-yong was born in 1943 and is arguably Korea's most renowned author. In 1993, he was sentenced to seven years in prison for an unauthorised trip to the North to promote exchange between artists in North and South Korea. Five years later, he was released on a special pardon by the new president. The recipient of Korea's highest literary prizes and shortlisted for the Prix Femina Étranger, his novels and short stories are published in North and South Korea, Japan, China, France, Germany, and the United States. Other novels include *The Ancient Garden, The Story of Mister Han, The Guest, The Shadow of Arms, Familiar Things,* and *At Dusk.*

Scribe Publications
18–20 Edward St, Brunswick, Victoria 3056, Australia
3754 Pleasant Ave, Suite 100, Minneapolis, Minnesota 55409 USA

First published in Great Britain in 2015 by Periscope, an imprint
of Garnet Publishing Limited, 8 Southern Court, South Street,
Reading RG1 4QS
Published in Australia by Scribe 2015
Published in North America by Scribe 2019

Typeset in Adobe Garamond
Printed and bound in the UK by CPI Group (UK) Ltd, Croydon
CR0 4YY

Scribe Publications is committed to the sustainable use of natural
resources and the use of paper products made responsibly from those
resources.

9781947534544 (US edition)
9781925106534 (Australian edition)
9781925113730 (e-book)

A CiP entry for this title is available from the National Library of
Australia

scribepublications.com
scribepublications.com.au

PRINCESS BARI

HWANG SOK-YONG

SCRIBE
Melbourne • London

Many small stars fill the blue sky, and many worries fill our lives. **Jindo** *Arirang*

[Korean folk anthem, variation from the Jindo region in South Korea]

ONE

I was barely twelve when my family was split apart.

I grew up in Chongjin. We lived in a house at the top of a steep hill overlooking the sea. In the spring, clusters of azalea blossoms would poke out from among the dry weeds, elbowing each other for space in the vacant lots, and flare a deeper red in the glow of the morning and evening sun as Mount Gwanmo, still capped with snow and cloaked in clouds from the waist down, floated against the wide eastern sky. From the top of the hill, I watched the lumbering steel ships anchored in the water and the tiny fishing boats sluggishly making their way around them, the rattle of their engines just reaching my ears. Seagulls shattered the sunlight's reflection on the surface of the water, which glittered like fish scales, before wheeling off into the sun itself. I used to wait there for my father to come home from his job at the harbour office or for my mother to come back from market. I would leave the road, scramble up a steep slope and squat at the edge of the cliff, because it was a good spot to watch out for them, but also I just liked looking down at the sea.

We had a full house: Grandmother, Father, Mother, my six older sisters. Most of us had been born within a year or two of each other, which meant our mother was pregnant or nursing for practically fifteen years straight. The moment one girl popped out, she was waddling around with the next. My two oldest sisters never forgot the fear that filled our house each time our mother went into labour.

Luckily, Grandmother was by her side each time, acting as midwife. They told me our father used to pace back and forth and chain-smoke outside the door or out in the courtyard, but after the third girl was born, whenever our mother showed signs of going into labour, he stayed late at work instead and even volunteered for the night shift. The anger he'd been suppressing finally exploded when Sook, the fifth girl, was born. That morning, Mother and Grandmother were in the main room off the kitchen, bathing newborn Sook in a tub of warm water, when Father returned home from night duty. He opened the door, took one look inside, and said: 'What're we supposed to do with another of those?' He yanked little Sook from their arms and shoved her head under the water. Shocked, our grandmother hurriedly fished the baby from the tub. Sook didn't cry, but just spluttered and coughed instead as if she'd swallowed too much water and couldn't breathe. When the sixth girl, Hyun, was born, Jin, the oldest, wound up with a brass bowl of *kimchi* on her head as she was coming back from the outhouse just as our father vented his anger by tossing the breakfast tray into the courtyard.

So what do you figure happened when I was born? Jin told me: 'We all crowded into the corner of the kids' room and shivered in fear.' After they heard the newborn's first cry, Sun, my second-oldest sister, crept out to investigate, only to return pouting and crying.

'We're doomed! It's another girl.'

Jin warned everyone: 'Not a peep out of any of you, and don't even *think* about stepping foot out of this room until Father gets home.'

Grandmother, who caught me when I was born, wrapped me in a blanket, my skin still covered in blood and fluid, and then sat vacant-eyed on the dirt floor of the kitchen, too much at a loss to even think of boiling up a pot of seaweed soup for our mother. Mother cried quietly to herself; then, after a little while, she picked me up and carried me out of the house to a patch of woods a long way from our neighbourhood where no one ever went. There she tossed me into some dry underbrush among the pine trees, and covered my face with the blanket. She probably meant for me to smother to death, or to freeze in the cold morning wind.

When Father got home, he opened the door without a word. Of course, he could tell from the mood in the house — Mother had the blanket up over her face and was unresponsive, and Grandmother just coughed dryly now and then from her spot in the kitchen — that he had no hope of ever getting a son, and he turned heel and left. Mother and Grandmother each stayed put in their stupors, one inside and one out in the kitchen, until the sun was high in the sky. Finally, Grandmother went back inside.

'What happened to the baby?'

'Don't know. Must've crawled away on its own.'

3

'Why, you threw it out! You'll be struck dead by lightning for this, you stupid girl!'

Grandmother searched the house inside and out, but I was nowhere to be found. Fearful of how Heaven might curse them, and filled with pity for her daughter-in-law and poor little granddaughters, she filled a porcelain bowl with cold water, placed it on a small, legged tray and sat out back, rubbing her palms together in prayer.

'Gods on Earth, gods in Heaven, I pray to you, lift the bad fortune from this home, bring that baby back in one piece, turn the poor mother's heart, calm the father's anger and keep us all safe.'

Grandmother finished praying and searched the house again and all over the courtyard and the surrounding neighbourhood, before finally giving up and returning home. She sat despairingly on the *twenmaru*, the narrow wooden porch that lined the house, when our dog Hindungi suddenly poked her head out of the doghouse and stared up at her. As Grandmother turned to look at the dog, her eye caught a tiny corner of the blanket she'd wrapped me in. Hoping against hope, she dashed over to the doghouse and peeked inside: Hindungi was lying down, and there I was, bundled up and nestled between her paws. Grandmother said my eyes were closed, and I was snuffling in my sleep. Hindungi must have followed our mother when she left the house to get rid of me, slinking behind at a careful distance, and then caught my scent and hunted through the underbrush before picking me up in her jaws and carrying me home.

'*Aigo*, our Hindungi is such a good dog! This child was

sent to us from Heaven, I'm sure of it!'

Maybe that's why I felt closest to my grandmother and our dog when I was little. Hindungi was named for the white fur that her breed, Pungsan, was known for, but I myself didn't have a name until my hundredth day, when babies are said to be fully among the living and I was sure to survive infancy. It hadn't occurred to anyone to give me one. Later, after our family was dispersed in all directions and my grandmother and I were living in that dugout hut on the other side of the Tumen River, she told me a story she'd heard long, long ago from her great-grandmother. It was the story of Princess Bari, whose name meant 'abandoned'. She would always finish the story by singing the last lines to me:

'"*Throw her out, the little throwaway. Cast her out, the little castaway.*" So that's how you got the name "Bari".'

In any case, for a long time I didn't have a name. Grandmother brought it up while we were eating one day. We were sitting at the round tray with Mother, after Father and Grandmother were served their food at the square tray.

'I mean, really!' Grandmother confronted Father out of the blue. 'Why doesn't that baby have a name yet?'

Father slowly ran his eyes over the children clustered around the table, as if counting us one by one.

'Well,' he said, 'I know there are enough girl names for twins, all the way up to sextuplets … but what am I supposed to do after that? I only know so many characters.'

'You mean to say you went to college and can speak Chinese *and* Russian, but you can't come up with a name for your baby girl?'

This was back when the Republic was still generous,

so whenever twins were born, regardless of whether they were in a big city or a remote country village, reporters would show up from the TV stations and newspapers and the babies would appear on the evening news. Thanks to the country's strong welfare system, babies were cared for in state nurseries and mothers received ample rations of powdered formula, and the Great Leader himself would thank the parents and shower them with gifts, from baby clothes to toys. Quadruplet girls were named after the four noble plants of classical Chinese art — Orchid, Bamboo, Chrysanthemum, and Plum Blossom — and there were probably similar matching names for quintuplets and sextuplets. That's what our father meant when he said he had only been prepared for six girls. My sisters' names — Jin, Sun, Mi (Truth, Goodness, and Beauty) and Jung, Sook, Hyun (Grace, Virtue, and Wisdom) — came in sets of three, and no more. Our father probably thought that my being born a girl had turned those complete and perfectly matched names into a meaningless jumble of letters. He had nothing more to say about it. But since the subject had been raised, Grandmother and Mother kept talking after he left for work.

'Little Mother, maybe it's time we gave it a name,' Grandmother said.

'Name her "Sorry" or "Letdown", because that's how I feel. Sorry and let down.'

'I *have* heard of names like that before, but let's see. You tried to abandon her in the woods ...'

And that's how my grandmother came up with my name. Of course, it wasn't until much later, after I'd gone to the ends of the Earth and suffered every kind of hardship, that I understood exactly why she named me 'Bari'.

—

Our father was raised by his widowed mother. Grandfather died in a war that started long before I was born. Grandmother claims he was a war hero, and that his story had even made its way onto one of the central radio station's broadcasts. In some faraway seaside town way down in the south, Grandfather had fought off a troop of Big Noses, and singlehandedly at that, as they were rolling in on their tanks. Grandmother would often retell the story after dinner when the trays had been put away, or on summer nights when we would spread out straw mats in the front courtyard and gaze up at the stars. But one night Father got so fed up with hearing it that he butted in, and the heroic tale of my grandfather lost its shine.

'Enough already! Stop it with your stories. That's all straight out of a Soviet film.'

'What film?'

'That film we saw in town. Don't you remember? The neighbourhood unit went to see it as a group. You're mixing it up with Father's story.'

The plot of the film went like this: a young soldier, still wet behind the ears, falls asleep while standing guard beneath a collapsed building in a shelled-out city. At dusk, his unit retreats, leaving him behind and still fast asleep. Meanwhile, enemy troops roll right in under the assumption that the ruined city has been evacuated. The soldier is startled awake by the noise. He sees tanks, the headlights of army vehicles, and the shadowy figures of enemy soldiers coming down the main strip. Terrified, he aims his submachine gun, pauses in absolute bewilderment and pulls the trigger. The tanks stop, and for a moment all is silent. The soldiers halt in unison, then turn and retreat: they believe their enemy is waiting to ambush them in the dark. Only then does the soldier crawl out from the rubble and take off running. He runs all night, and manages to catch up to his unit around daybreak. He's called before the platoon leader, then the company commander, and finally the general, who praise him each in turn and later bestow him with a medal. He's named a hero for singlehandedly stopping an enemy division, and is rewarded with a special furlough.

Anyway, from what our father told us, it was probably true that Grandfather had been killed in combat on the eastern front. He said Grandmother was called before the People's Committee and given official notification of his death along with some extra rations in recognition of his services, and when Father went to school, his homeroom teacher had him stand at the podium while she made the students offer up a moment of silence. But Grandmother had already known exactly when Grandfather had died, and had fixed the date for the anniversary of his death so the family would know when to observe memorial rites every year. As always, she had seen what was coming in her dreams.

Late one night, Grandmother heard Grandfather's familiar cough outside and opened the door. A ray of moonlight shone down on the courtyard, and in it stood Grandfather in a torn military uniform. She asked him where he'd been, and he said he'd walked up the east coast, through the towns of Mukho, Gangneung, Sokcho, over twenty mountains, maybe more, to get to her. He was carrying a bundle of some sort under his arm, so she told him to set it on the *twenmaru* and come on in, that she would make breakfast for him in the morning; but he said he had a long way to go still, and he kept his shoes on and remained standing. Grandmother quickly took his bundle and set it down, but when she turned back, he had vanished. The courtyard was empty. She awoke with a start and put her hand out. There was something on the floor next to the bedding. When she turned on the lamp to examine it, the wardrobe doors were hanging open and some clothes had spilled out: Grandfather's padded pants and jacket and the rabbit-fur-lined vest he had taken off and stashed in the closet before leaving for the army. That night, she hastily scrounged together a bottle of alcohol, dried pollock, and some fruit for his memorial table to give him a simple sending off, and burned his clothes to send him on his way.

Grandmother saw ghosts sometimes, and could even hear the nonsensical conversations they had. Ever since our father was young, she would set out a bowl of clean, freshly drawn well water behind the house and pray before it to the gods, but after such things were outlawed by the Republic, she stopped doing it outside and would squat on the dirt floor of the kitchen and pray there instead. Mother and Father tried to stop her at first, and the two of them would get into fights about it.

'Aren't you supposed to stop her when she starts up with that black magic?'

'*Aigo*! Do you really think your mother's going to listen to me? She scares me with all that ghost talk. I don't dare say a word about it. Besides … doesn't it run in your family?'

'What do you mean, "runs in my family"?'

'Well, she said your great-great-grandmother was a shaman in Hamheung.'

'Watch your mouth! Don't you know what kind of trouble we could get in if you start spreading that nonsense around?'

'But when I married you, everyone in your village knew that your great-grandmother and your great-great-grandmother were powerful shamans before Liberation …'

'Damn it, woman! Keep it down! We're descended from poor farmers. That means we're part of the core class.'

Grandmother said that Father had been a good student ever since his days at the People's Primary School. Right after the war, when the Chinese People's Volunteer Army was still stationed in the city, he had picked up some Chinese here and there and would even go to the base with the older folk to help settle civil complaints. He graduated first in his class from secondary school and even received a recommendation to attend university in Pyongyang.

Our parents wound up married to each other due to our grandmother's meddling. Father had completed his labour mobilisation during summer break from his first year of university, and found a spare week to return home for a visit only to discover a girl waiting there for him.

He stepped through the gate and called out: 'Mother, can you bring me some cold water?' Who should come out of the kitchen then but this short, bob-haired girl carrying a bowl of water with both hands …

He forgot all about the water and stared at her stupidly before finally asking: 'Who're you, Comrade?'

Grandmother answered for her.

'Who do you think? That's your wife.'

Father practically jumped out of his skin at that and ran for the station, where he hopped the first train for Pyongyang. About a month later, he was ordered to report to the academic affairs office. The professor in charge of monitoring the students stood with his cheeks puffed out and studied him for a moment, before gesturing with his chin for him to sit down.

'I didn't think you were the type, Comrade — only a student, but already you're married … Now, I know your mother's a widow and girls run in your family, so I understand why you want to get started as soon as possible and try for a son. But explain to me why you abandoned your wife.'

Father, flabbergasted, started talking gibberish.

'No, uh, it's not like that, you see, I went home for a short visit and out of the blue my mother said I was married so I hurried back to school and —'

Just then the door cracked open, and Grandmother stuck her head in.

'Hey! We're here,' she said, and stepped inside. Then she glanced back at someone and said: 'Well, come in already.'

The bob-haired girl followed her in, head hanging down, and bowed wordlessly at the professor. Father's face turned bright red. He got up without saying a word.

'We don't need to discuss this any further,' the professor

said. 'I'll issue you a pass so you can escort your mother home. You're married now. Time to go home and consummate it.'

'I have to finish school first …'

'You should've thought about that before you got married! Go on, now. If you stick around any longer, I'll have to tell your comrades. If the Youth Association gets wind of this, you'll be marked as a bad element, maybe even as a decadent, and you'll be expelled.'

So that was how Father wound up being dragged back to Chongjin. From the moment they boarded the train, Grandmother started laying down threats.

'No more running around from now on. This union was arranged by my guardian spirit, so if you don't do as I say, we're through. You'll go your way, and I'll go mine.'

Grandmother produced a baby sling from somewhere and tied one end around Father's leg where he was sitting. Then she tied a round knot into the sling and held it up to Mother's ankle.

'Lift your foot, girl. Slip it through this.'

Mother took off her rubber shoe, pulled up her sagging sock, and said: 'Make it tight.'

Father told us that when he turned his head to see what the two women were doing, Mother met his eye and stuck her tongue out at him. (Right up until we were all separated, any time that story happened to come up when they were fighting, Father would burst out: 'I should've chopped my leg off and run away to start a new life back when I had the chance!') Grandmother wrapped the free end of the sling around her wrist several times and then let out a long sigh, as if she could finally relax. At this point in the story, my sisters and I would ask her: 'Why did you decide to make Mother your daughter-in-law?' Grandmother would tell us about the dream she'd had, and how she had gone to our mother's village to find her.

'I dreamed that a celestial maiden fell out of the sky and landed with a loud thud right on top of the house. She rolled off the roof and into the courtyard. I called out: "Hello, hello, if you're a ghost, then back off, and if you're a person, then be on your way." But she told me she had tended the garden of the Great Jade Emperor in his heavenly palace, and that she'd been dropped to Earth as punishment for overwatering the flowers and causing them to fall from their stems.

'I glanced around the courtyard, and sure enough, there were exactly seven flowers lying on the ground. She picked them up one by one and offered them to me. I put out my hand to take them, but before I could, that crazy girl opened the gate and took a hop, skip, and a jump backwards and ran off. I ran after her. I chased her all the way to a sorghum-stalk fence in front of someone's house, and then I woke up.

'The dream was so strange that I went outside to take a look. The road the celestial maiden had taken led to the next village. I wound my way down the road just like I had in the dream, and ended up at a house surrounded by a sorghum-stalk fence and thought: *How curious is this?* When I went into the yard, a girl was singing. She was wiping down the large clay jars on the *jangdokdae*. She had cleaned the soybean paste jars and soy sauce jars to a high shine. From behind, she had a nice rump, and though I'm a woman myself and not a man, that butt of hers was as plump and tantalising as a peony. So I invited her to come and live with us. I met her parents too and told them all about your father.'

Everyone in the family knew that Grandmother had a strange gift, but Father alone refused to acknowledge it. Nevertheless, whenever it was the end of the year or the start of a new one, or when he woke up in the morning from an unsettling dream, he would stealthily ask her what his fortune held. 'Oh, and then,' he would mutter, as if to himself, 'this water jar split in two, and a catfish the size of my forearm came wriggling out.'

But not only would Grandmother *not* interpret his dream for him, she would toy with him by playing stupid: 'Mm, we should boil up some catfish stew! Give the whole family a feast.'

Since our mother kept winding up pregnant with another of us while she was still struggling to recover from the last pregnancy and take care of the latest newborn, she wasn't able to go to work like the other mothers. Our parents must have been more careful after Mi, the third girl, was born, because it was three years before Jung came along. Mother used that time to finally get out of the house. She helped with making side dishes in one of the food factories that had started on the collective farms and in cities and counties across the country during the postwar recovery years; then, later, she was assigned to a recreation centre where she learned hair cutting and styling techniques. After six months, she worked in the barbershop of a public bath in the city.

But because of Father's and Grandmother's unquenchable desire for a son and grandson, Mother was only able to work for about a year, including her apprenticeship period, before she had to quit. After the incident where Father held Sook under the bathwater, Mother seemed to give up entirely on the idea of doing something different with her life. Everyone said Sook wound up the way she did after having the measles, but Mother and Grandmother blamed Father for it and talked behind his back about how it was his fault for holding the newborn under water. Up until she'd passed her third birthday, it seemed as if she was just slow to start talking, but then they realised she'd been a deaf-mute all along.

—

I was attending a local kindergarten at the time, so I must have been about five years old. The azaleas had bloomed a bright red at the top of the hill, and my sisters were out filling their baskets with freshly-picked shepherd's purse, which means it had to be early spring.

I was sitting on the sunny *twenmaru* porch just off the main room, basking in the warm sun, when Hindungi suddenly crossed the courtyard, heading straight for the front gate and growling. Her ears were folded back, and she bared her teeth and started barking ferociously. Wondering who it was, I went over to the gate and pushed open the wooden door. A little girl, just a bit bigger than me, was standing there. She wore a shin-length *mongdang* skirt and a *jeogori* blouse, both made from white cotton. I thought she was one of Hyun's friends coming over to play. I said: 'Hyun's not home right now,' but the girl just stared straight

15

at me without saying a word. Hindungi was still barking wildly behind me, but the girl didn't look the least bit scared.

I thought I heard her say: 'This isn't the place.' No sooner did I hear those words than she turned and ran off. Actually, I'm not sure whether she ran away or faded away right before my eyes. I hurried out the gate, wondering where she'd vanished to, and saw that she was already way down at the far end of the path that ran along the other houses, which were all similar in size and shape to ours. Her ponytail swayed back and forth as she went. She stopped in front of a house with an apricot tree in the yard, turned to look my way, and slipped inside. The reason I remember that ponytail is because of the bright red ribbon fluttering at the end of it. That night, while we were all eating dinner, our mother told Father there'd been a death in the neighbourhood.

'We need to give some condolence money to the head of the neighbourhood unit. Her family just lost their grandson.'

'What? How did he die?'

Before Mother could answer Father's question, Grandmother muttered to herself: 'Must have been something in his past life. It's fate.'

'You don't think it's the typhoid fever that's been going around?'

I tugged on the hem of Grandmother's skirt to tell her what I'd seen earlier.

'Grandma! Grandma!'

'Yes, yes, let's eat.'

'I saw something earlier, Grandma. A little girl came to our door and then left. She went into the house with the apricot tree in the yard.'

16

No one paid any attention, but after dinner Grandmother pulled me aside, sat me down on the *twenmaru* and asked me a lot of questions.

'Who did you say you saw?'

'A little girl dressed all in white. Hindungi barked at her and tried to bite her. When she saw me, she said, "This isn't the place," and left. I wondered where she was going so I followed her outside, and I saw her go into the apricot-tree house.'

'Did you make eye contact with her?'

'Yes! Right before she went in, she turned and looked at me.'

Grandmother nodded and stroked my hair.

'You'll be all right,' she said. 'You've got the gift in your blood. Now, do as Grandmother tells you. Spit on the ground three times and stamp your left foot three times.'

That day I became very ill. My body got really hot, and I started talking nonsense. It went on all night. Father carried me on his back to a hospital down near the harbour. Children and old people who'd been brought there from towns and villages nearby were lying in rows in every room. I don't remember how many days I spent there. All I do remember is seeing that little girl perched on the ledge of the lattice window, close to where several people were lying. I stared up at her. I wasn't afraid. After I was sent home, my sisters were moved out of the back room where we normally all slept, and my grandmother stayed by my side. She was the only one who would come near me. My fever would dip during the day and then set me afire again at night. Hives the size of millet seeds broke out all over my body and took

17

a long time to go away. Grandmother kept asking me about the girl.

'Do you still see her?'

'No, but I did at the hospital. Grandma, who is she?'

'That's the typhoid ghost. Nothing will happen to you. My guardian spirit is keeping watch.'

I don't know how long I was sick. I kept slipping in and out of sleep both day and night. I can still remember the dream I had:

I enter the grounds of what looks like an old temple. A stone wall has collapsed, and tiles from the half-caved-in roof lie scattered about in the reedy, weed-filled courtyard. I don't go into the darkened temple, but instead stand nervously next to a slanting pillar and peer inside. Something moves. A dark red ribbon comes slithering out of the shadows. I turn and start to run. The ribbon stands on end and springs after me. I run through a forest, wade across a stream and cut through rice paddies, clambering over the high ridges between them, and make it back to the entrance of our village. The whole time, that red ribbon is dancing after me. Just then, Grandmother appears. She looks different — she's wearing a white *hanbok* and has her hair up in a chignon with a long hairpin holding it in place. She pushes me behind her and lets out a loud yell:

'Hex, be gone!'

The ribbon slithers to the ground and vanishes.

I woke up in a panic. My body and face were drenched in sweat as if I'd been caught in a rainstorm. Grandmother sat up and wiped my face and neck with a cotton cloth. 'Hold on just a little longer, and it'll pass,' she said.

Though I was awake, my body kept growing and shrinking over and over as the fever rose and fell. My arms and legs grew longer and longer until they were pressed up against the floor and the walls. Then they shrivelled and shrank up smaller than beans, like rolled up balls of snot dug from both nostrils, and got softer and softer until the skin burst. The warm floor against my back dropped and carried me down, down, down, into the earth below. Faces appeared in the wallpaper. Their mouths opened, and they laughed and chattered noisily at me.

I made it through the typhoid fever, but for several years, right up until I started school, I remained frail. I started hearing things I hadn't heard before and seeing things that weren't there before. That was also when I started communicating with our mute sister, Sook. Jung, the fourth-oldest, and Sook, the fifth, were only a year apart and were always at each other's throats. It was the same with Hyun and me — as she was the second-youngest after me, I never bothered treating her like an older sister and she was always irritated with me because of it. Jin, Sun, and Mi were much older than the rest of us, and they were bigger too. After all, a good three years separated Mi and the next one down, Jung. Anyway, Hyun and I were both treated like babies by everyone else, but Jung and Sook were awkwardly positioned in the family. Whenever an errand had to be run, it always fell to them. Between the two of them, Jung was the easier mark. Since Sook couldn't talk, there was a limit to what she could be ordered to do. For instance, if you told them to run down to the greengrocer at the bottom of the hill and bring back some tofu and green onions, Jung would push her bottom lip out and glare menacingly at Sook.

'I get stuck having to do everything because of *her*.'

Because she couldn't communicate through words, Sook was short-tempered. She would get along with everyone fine for a while, doing what she was told, but the moment she lost her temper she was ripping out clumps of hair and kicking at stomachs — big sister, little sister, none of that mattered when she was on the attack. For that reason, our parents did their best to treat Jung and Sook equally. When they bought us clothes, Jung and Sook were given identical styles and patterns, and even pencils were doled out in identical sets of three.

One morning, my sisters were running around getting ready for school, taking turns going to the toilet, washing their faces, and combing their hair when Sook began to shriek. Her face turned bright red from screaming, but since she couldn't speak, no one knew what was wrong. She was holding something in her hand and shaking it: a single scorched trainer. It seemed that the trainer, which had been washed the night before and set on top of the warm, wood-burning stove to dry, had fallen in front of the open flames. Naturally, Sook and Jung wore identical blue trainers. Clever Jung had snatched up the unscathed pair and put them on, claiming they were hers, and left the burned shoe where she'd found it. Sook threw the burned shoe and hurled herself at Jung, grabbing her around the waist and tackling her. Jung squirmed and struggled as Sook pulled the undamaged shoes off Jung's feet. That was her way of saying they were hers. Unwilling to admit defeat, Jung bit her arm. Their screaming and crying shook the whole neighbourhood. Father, who was steaming with anger, changed his mind about leaving for work and made them line up at the edge of the *twenmaru* so he could take a switch to their calves.

'Not a moment's peace in this house on account of you two girls!'

The morning had been ruined for everyone; the entire family stood and watched as Father hit the girls on the calves with the switch. But right then, I heard Sook's voice inside my head: *But it* was *Jung's. Her shoes were on top of the stove. Mine were by the gate. The neighbour's cat has been sneaking into the kitchen to steal dried fish. I saw the cat run off with one last night.* I unconsciously babbled these words, which were buzzing in my ears. Father paused and Grandmother went to check the top of the cupboard next to the stove.

'What happened to that dried pollock I was planning to add to the soup?' she asked.

Relieved, Mother grabbed the switch away from Father and said: 'See? It's the cat's fault.'

Father muttered something about 'too many damn girls killing me with all this racket' as he picked up his files and documents one by one and left for work, while Grandmother comforted Jung and Sook.

'Why don't we ask your father to buy you two some new shoes on his way home from work? Hurry on to school now.'

After my sisters had all gone, and I was the only one left

at home, Mother said: 'Well, that was strange. How did she figure out what Sook was trying to say?'

'What'd I tell you? Our Bari inherited the gift.'

Mother blanched.

'Please,' she said, 'don't ever mention those old wives' tales of yours in front of their father.'

TWO

One day, I think around the time I started school, Hindungi met up with a boy dog and got pregnant, despite being, as Grandmother put it, well into her old-lady years. The grown-ups all clucked their tongues and exclaimed what a disgrace it was, but Hindungi strutted about the courtyard, her sagging belly and teats swaying. She gave birth late one winter night when no one was looking. We were all lying in a row beneath the blankets when we overheard Grandmother and Mother whispering outside the door.

'How many are there?' Grandmother asked.

'One … two … three … What the —! *Seven!*'

'Will wonders never cease? They say flowers can bloom on an old tree, and sure enough this old granny's had herself seven babies.'

The next morning, before Mother could come in, pull back our blankets and smack us on the butt to tell us to hurry, get up, get ready for school, we all rose at once. Some of us rushed to change clothes first while the others spilled out into the courtyard in our long underwear. As we crowded in front of the doghouse like a school of minnows at the water's edge, fighting over who would get to stick her face in the tiny doorway first, Hindungi — who had always been so gentle with us — stuck her head out the doorway, bared her teeth, and growled. Mother warned us to back away.

'Give her space. She's worried you'll hurt her babies.'

When my older sisters took a hesitant step back, I saw my chance to get a peek inside, so I crouched down in front of the doghouse. Then, with my mouth firmly shut, I spoke inside my head: *It's me. Bari. The seventh. Don't worry. I just wanted to see my little brothers and sisters.*

Then, would you believe it? Hindungi staggered to her feet and stepped right out of the doghouse. The puppies, so tiny they could have fit inside my own tiny hand, were clustered together with their eyes shut tight on scraps of straw sacks. I stuck my hand into that warm puppy pile, gently pulled one out and cradled it against my chest. I could feel its heart beating softly against my fingertips. *So you're the seventh one too, just like me*, I thought.

I was so engrossed with the puppy in my arms that I forgot anyone else was even there. When I finally looked back, Mother, Grandmother, and all my sisters were standing in a semi-circle around me, staring silently down at the puppy and me. Even Father was standing at the edge of the *twenmaru* in a daze, but then he broke the silence.

'Don't tell me they're all girls, too.'

'Hey, hey,' Grandmother shook a broom at him. 'Don't ruin the morning with your grumbling.'

My sisters went back to arguing and crowding around the doorway to the doghouse, but Hindungi growled and blocked them with her body. Jung raised her hand as if to hit the dog.

'You stupid dog, why are you playing favourites?'

Hindungi got angrier and started to bark loudly. I put the puppy I was holding back in the doghouse.

I'll keep you safe, I said inside my head.

Hindungi went back into the doghouse, tucked her babies between her legs and lay with her body curled around them. I could hear Jin, my oldest sister, muttering behind me: 'Bari is so weird. Now she's talking to dogs?'

No one had anything to say to that; at some point, they had all caught on to the fact that there was something different about me. But no one, not even Mother and Father, ever said anything out loud about my behaviour, because Grandmother would glare at them and take my side. That day stands out in my memory, but how I met Chilsung — the youngest of Hindungi's litter — is only part of the story. You see, that was also the day our mother's brother came to town.

Hyun and I were playing marbles in the courtyard when the wooden gate cracked open and someone stuck their head in and peered around. We took one look at that grown-up head, with its shaved hair on top of what had to be a very tall, gangly body, and we flung the marbles away and drew back to the far end of the *twenmaru*. Hyun was so scared that, although she refused to admit it later after we were all grown up, I was sure I saw pee trickling down her calves.

'Hey kids, where's your mother?'

Undaunted, I took a step forward and demanded: 'Who're you?'

He peered around the courtyard some more and then stuck his whole upper body inside the gate.

'Assuming this is the right house, I might be your uncle.'

Mother, who'd been preparing dinner, stepped out of the kitchen as if on cue and ran over with her arms open.

'*Aigo*, look who's here! When did you get into town? Are you on leave?'

At last our uncle stepped all the way into the courtyard, clasped our mother's outstretched hands and gave them a shake.

'I'm out of the army now. How's my brother-in-law …?'

'He'll be home soon. Come sit.'

He was dressed in an old, faded work uniform and carried a canvas rucksack and an accordion. Before following our mother into the house, he gave each of us, still cowering in fright, a rough tousle on the head. He probably meant for it to be an affectionate pat, but it made me angry. Much better were the gifts that came out of his rucksack later, but first he stuck his hand in his pocket and snickered.

'I picked up something for you on the way here.'

Our uncle opened his hand and a black something or other leaped out at us. I took a few steps back, but Hyun fell right on her butt and shrieked.

On the ground next to her was a huge toad the size of a grown man's fist. Its eyes bulging like brass bells, it inflated its throat and let out a loud *gwaak! gwaak!*. I grabbed Hyun under the armpits and dragged her away — her eyes had rolled up inside her head, and the whites were showing. Mother ran over and scooped Hyun up into her arms.

'Just got here, and already you're causing trouble!

When're you going to grow up?' Our uncle snorted with laughter and tousled my hair again. Later, when he handed out the military hardtack and jawbreakers he had stuffed in his rucksack to us as a show of apology and reconciliation, Hyun refused to eat any of it and sat as far away from him as possible. Even when he gave an exciting performance on the accordion in a second attempt to befriend his little nieces, Hyun would only watch indifferently from the other side of the door.

Our uncle lived with us for several months until he found a job, and I got to know him a little better. He was good at the accordion. He was well known back in secondary school for his performances in the school band, and even in the army, instead of having to do labour, he was sent from base to base to perform propaganda songs for the soldiers. Every time he leaned up against the wall of the house and played his accordion, one leg splayed and stamping out a rhythm against the ground, all the neighbourhood kids came swarming. His eyes would flutter as he lost himself in the music, shoulders rising and falling as he filled the bellows with air and pushed it out again. Our father would take one look at that and grumble to Mother:

'He's got no sense. Who'd want to employ a joker like him?'

'Someone will. Everyone says he's bright and has a good personality.'

With Father's help and the recommendations of several members of our neighbourhood unit, our uncle got a job at a trading company.

During my second year in school, things started to go

downhill. It wasn't just our family but the entire city of Chongjin. The grown-ups whispered among themselves that even Pyongyang was worse off than it had ever been. The cookies and candies that had been distributed to children on every holiday and at every memorial were, of course, cut off, and our rations of white rice were mixed with chopped-up corn until the rice gradually ran out; there were more and more months when we received only corn.

Oh! I have to tell you what happened to Hindungi, her puppies, and little Chilsung. I told you that Hindungi had seven babies. Well, despite our attempts to stop her, our mother couldn't stand the sight of those squirming pups, so she put them in a basket to take to market. I happened to be coming home from school just as she was leaving, and I clung to the basket with both hands and shook my head and cried.

'No, you can't!'

'Child, how are we supposed to raise *seven* dogs? I've got my hands full already trying to keep you girls fed.'

'Grandma, stop her!'

Grandmother came running out and tried to calm us down: 'How about if we keep just one dog and sell the others?'

I chose Chilsung because he and I had been friends from the start. Mother tried to snatch him back, but Grandmother put her arm around my shoulders and turned me away from her. The whole time our mother was collecting the puppies, Hindungi lay slumped in her doghouse and didn't budge. They were ready to be weaned, after all, and besides, Hindungi knew it was coming.

28

One day, around the time that Chilsung's legs had just grown long and his ears were standing up, Mama Hindungi disappeared. Of course, by that I mean that Mother and Grandmother gave her to someone, not that she left on her own. Hindungi was moving sluggishly with age and had some kind of skin disorder: the hair on her rump had fallen out and the pink skin underneath was showing. Bathing the dog in water used to boil adzuki beans was supposed to help, but by then we were well into the days when such things as rice cakes piled high with the sweet mashed beans were a thing of the past, so how were we supposed to find so much as a single adzuki bean? I no longer resent my uncle, but back then, after hearing that he was the one who'd dragged Hindungi away, I stopped offering him any nice words in response to anything he tried to say to me. (That wasn't the only reason. It didn't happen until much later, but he was also the reason our family became split up.) Grandmother told me what happened when Hindungi left.

'Your uncle said he would give her to some men he works with. She must be at least fifteen years old now — that's a long life for a dog. How can we bear to watch her suffer? So I told him to take her. When your uncle put the rope leash on her, she fought it and dug in her heels. I stroked her head to calm her down and told her: 'You're sick. He's taking you somewhere to make you all better, so go on.' That's when she gave in and tottered after him. But she kept looking back at me after every few steps.'

When we heard that Hindungi had followed our uncle because Grandmother told her he was taking her to get healed, but still had to be dragged away because she suspected it wasn't true, my sisters and I turned our backs on our grandmother and burst into tears. There was no mystery about what middle-aged men planned to do with an old dog. They would gather on a riverbank somewhere, pass around bottles of cheap *soju*, light a bonfire, fill a big iron pot with water and get it boiling as they laughed and cackled …

Fortunately, we still had Chilsung. Grandmother had named him after the seven stars in the Big Dipper, because he was the seventh pup, just like me. He took his mother's place in the old doghouse, and from then on luck began to smile on us. Of course, it wasn't all good news: our uncle got out of the army and came back. Jin got married and moved to Wonsan, and Sun enlisted in the army, which was good — but the best thing by far that happened to us was that our father got promoted and we moved into a new house. Mother and Grandmother were so delighted that they never once got annoyed while packing our things. They went along with whatever Father wanted, and didn't raise their voices at us either.

Chongjin had always been known as the best city to live in. The high mountains that surrounded the city like a folding screen blocked the cold north winds and kept us in firewood, wild greens, and all kinds of fruit; delicious rice grew in fields fed by the Suseong Stream, which never dried up even during the worst droughts; and the waters were rich with seafood, which was why, whenever I told people from other parts of the country that I was from Chongjin, they said: 'Ah, you grew up in Paradise.'

But best of all, it wasn't too far from the border, which

meant there was a frequent exchange of goods, and even ordinary citizens could easily get their hands on things from the outside world. Sons and daughters who'd moved to other parts of the country after getting married used to send word to their families in Chongjin asking them to buy various items for them from over the border. But once rumours started going around that the Soviet Union had collapsed some years earlier, the grown-ups began whispering about the poor shape the Republic was in. Chongjin had it better than other cities, though not as good as Pyongyang, of course; even so, there were times when rations were cut off for two months and then three months, and shabbily dressed people who'd left the countryside in search of food began showing up in the market streets.

Father became a vice chairman in Musan. The city of Musan produced a lot of iron ore and coal and various minerals, and our mother boasted proudly over and over that there was no one better suited than our father at trading the seafood that came out of Chongjin and the minerals that came out of Musan with China in exchange for food. That was probably because Father had worked in the trade sector since he was young and, as Grandmother liked to brag, Chinese and Russian flowed from his mouth like water.

The Party chartered a truck to haul our belongings to Chongjin Station, but in fact our luggage was minimal given the size of our family. All we had packed was bedding, a big bundle of clothes, pots and pans, and the like. As the company housing came furnished with cupboards and wardrobes, we gave those items to our neighbours and asked our uncle to sell the electrical appliances, such as our fan, refrigerator, and

31

black-and-white television. According to our uncle, Father would be posted right on the border, so we would be able to buy the latest models very cheaply. The truck was necessary simply because there were so many of us.

A bit of trouble arose when we put Chilsung in the back. The young Party worker sitting with Father in the cab of the truck objected: 'What're you packing the dog for? You should give it to your neighbours. It'll go good with some alcohol.'

'You're right. But the kids have been raising it like it's part of the family …'

I was crouching right behind the cab, holding on tight to Chilsung, so I heard everything they were saying. Judging by the worried looks on their faces, my sisters heard them too. Our mother shook her finger at me, and Grandmother pulled a skirt out from the bundle of clothes and tossed it over. She meant for me to cover Chilsung up with it.

'There are a lot of starving families in the mountains. How is this going to reflect on you, Comrade Vice Chairman?'

'I understand what you're saying. Once we get to Musan, we'll decide whether to keep it or give it away.'

I had not forgotten the promise I'd made to Chilsung the day the puppies were born — that whisper inside my head when I said I would keep him safe.

The truck pulled into the train station, and we were directed by a station employee to board the empty passenger car first while our belongings were loaded into the open-air freight car at the front of the train. Travel was still strictly regulated then, so it was an orderly process. Fewer travellers meant more available seats. Later, everything would fall apart: the aisles would be packed with people and the windows would all be smashed out.

As soon as we sat down, I pushed Chilsung under the seat and told him several times inside my head: *People will get angry if they see you. I know it's stuffy, but stay still under there.* Of course, Chilsung and I had been communicating with each other through our thoughts since he was a pup; he understood, and lay flat on his belly with his limbs stretched out and his head tucked down, just as if he were lying beneath the porch. Each time I leaned down to see how he was doing, he hadn't budged in the slightest except for his gently wagging tail.

—

Musan sat at the centre of a wide plain, surrounded by hills on all sides; across the Tumen River to the north, a steep mountain on the Chinese side rose straight up like a wall. We unpacked our belongings in the company housing, which was at the northern end of the city near the government office.

One day — probably in the early summer, the year our Great Leader died — we returned home from school and my sisters and I followed Mi down to the river to wash clothes. Freight trucks were leaving the customs office and heading across the plain for downtown Musan.

'*Ya, ya!* A Chinese car!' Mi yelled. 'A Chinese car! Pack up the laundry.'

We gave the laundry we were swirling around in the

water a quick wringing and stuffed it in the basket, and then we all took off running.

'Here comes Uncle Salamander!'

Jung clapped her hands and skipped. Although Sook couldn't give voice to it, she was so excited that she ran ahead of the pack. I kept stopping to wait for Hyun and to help her up each time she sank to the ground, too winded to keep up.

'Can't you run any faster?'

'My heart feels like it's going to explode.'

When our house was finally visible in the distance, we all slowed to a walk and caught our breath. Uncle Salamander was a department head for a Chinese company in Yanji. He was short, chubby, and had a potbelly, and his eyes were big and round like a startled rabbit's, so you couldn't help but laugh just to look at him. His real name was Pak Xiaolong, and he and our uncle had gotten to know each other while doing business in Chongjin. Chinese companies both big and small would bring over things like corn or flour or even the occasional rice or clothes and sundry goods, and trade them for seafood or minerals.

Mr Pak got the nickname 'Salamander' because of a joke our father had made. A few days after we'd moved in, Mr Pak had come to our house, saying that he wanted to meet his comrade, the vice chairman. He'd brought a case of *kaoliang* liquor and two sides of pork ribs, and he must have heard there were a lot of kids in our family because he also brought two gift boxes filled with all kinds of cookies and candies. His visits, which reminded me of Grandmother's tales of club-wielding *dokkaebi* — goblins that sometimes surprised people with gifts instead of pranks — also inspired Mother and Grandmother to go on and on about how great it was to live near the border and praise our father all the more for his promotion.

People came from the maritime customs office and the People's Committee, and an oil drum with the top cut off was filled with charcoal and used to barbecue the ribs in the courtyard. After a few rounds of drinks, Mr Pak seemed to take an instant liking to our father, because he went from calling him 'Comrade Vice Chairman' to 'Father Vice Chairman' and then, after they'd talked some more, simply 'Elder Brother'. At any rate, it was true what people said about Mr Pak: he had an unusual knack for getting close to people he'd just met.

'Don't worry, Elder Brother. I may not look like much now, but I was an officer in the Chinese army. I served in Kunming, right on the border of Vietnam. There's no part of China I haven't been to. So if you need anything at all, just say the word. I may not be able to find you monkey horns or girl testicles, but I *can* bring you things that North Korea at least has never seen or even heard of.'

Father cocked his head, shot glass in hand.

'You say your name is ... Xiaolong? That means "Little Dragon", right? But you're built more like a toad than a dragon ...'

'Ah, what're you talking about, Elder Brother? Nowadays I spend all my time going back and forth across the Tumen, but in my younger days, I was stick-thin and so good-looking that I almost became a movie star!'

'Oh, now I know. Since your name means "little dragon",

35

that makes you a salamander!'

Everyone at the party had a good laugh, and the word *salamander* spread through the crowd. After that, Mr Pak lost his real name and became known as 'Uncle Salamander' to everyone from the customs clerks and officers right down to us kids. Whenever we saw him loading and unloading goods with those bulging eyes of his, we couldn't help but burst into giggles, even when the situation demanded that we maintain decorum.

While stocking the warehouse behind the company housing, Uncle Salamander also stocked our house full of gifts. He brought our family sacks of flour and rice; and mooncakes, candy, and chocolate snack cakes for us kids to munch on. Mother tore a dried pollock into strips and served it with *soju*, and Uncle Salamander and our father poured each other drinks while we got one chocolate snack cake each.

'Do you kids even know what a treat these are?' Uncle Salamander said. 'They come from the South. Grandmother, you should try one, too.'

Grandmother removed the plastic wrapper and took a bite out of the round, dark cake with soft marshmallow filling in the middle. Her eyes widened. 'Where'd you say you got this from?'

'South Korea, madam. Isn't it tasty, kids?'

We were too busy eating to answer. The flavour sent a jolt through me, from the tip of my tongue down to the bottom of my stomach. For days and weeks before Uncle Salamander appeared, we'd had nothing to eat but corn. At school, most of the students went without lunch, and rations for mine workers had already begun to be cut off for a couple of months at a time. Grain trucks would cross the river and head straight for Chongjin. They said there were a large number of remote mountain villages and backwoods towns by then with no one living in them. But since shipments of food passed through Musan, everyone was able to get by somehow, even if they had to miss a meal here and there.

Uncle Salamander lowered his voice and leaned closer to Father. 'The Republic will soon be better off,' he said.

'I don't know about that. The farms have been in turmoil for the last several years; the climate is changing. The Ryanggang Province highlands, for instance, used to be too cold to grow vegetables, but now I hear they have lettuce.'

'How are people supposed to live on lettuce? They should be growing potatoes. The problem is that the summer monsoons dump so much rain that all the crops — corn, potatoes, everything — gets washed away.'

'That's why the government keeps calling for the "great battle" to replace the topsoil, but no one actually cares enough to try. The earth is too thin for anything to grow.'

'Well, the government likes to throw around that bullshit about "self-reliance" and talk up the virtues of traditional farming, but all that really means is that they can't afford to modernise. You would need mountains of fertiliser over several years before you could coax anything out of that soil. But hey, at least on the outside, all the companies are hoping things will improve soon.'

'Why? Is something happening?'

'South and North ...' Uncle Salamander held his thumbs up next to each other. 'Face to face.'

'That is even less likely than Heaven being a real place.'

'No, it's true. I saw it on Chinese TV.'

'As if those Big Nose Yankees will ever let us be.'

'If North and South worked together instead of fighting each other, then everyone would be better off, and even we Korean-Chinese would be able to live free and proud.'

'You spin a good story.'

Then Uncle Salamander switched to Chinese, and Father responded and began speaking in Chinese as well, so we weren't able to follow their conversation.

A few days after Uncle Salamander left, Musan was turned inside out. Soldiers armed with rifles stood guard in every street, and the People's Committee building was turned into a funeral parlour. They told us the Great Leader had passed away suddenly. Schoolchildren were sent out in droves to the fields to pick all the wildflowers and make bouquets. We stood in line to enter the Committee building and offer up silent tribute before a photograph of the Great Leader. Every woman we ran across in the street, from teenagers to mothers to grandmothers, was weeping.

'Great Leader!' they cried. 'How can we go on without you ...?'

The city reverberated with the keening of mothers, who sat in groups on cement steps, their faces haggard. The little ones followed suit, even though they had no idea what was going on, crowding together in courtyards and in the middle of the street to weep, their tears mixing with sweat.

That summer was said to be one of the hottest in

decades. Not a drop of rain fell all season, but when autumn began it rained hard for several weeks in a row, until the fields and mountains had practically changed places. The grown-ups were used to fretting over poor crop yields, but that year a truly fearsome famine began. By winter, rations had been cut off in cities and provinces alike. That was also around the time that our mother's brother, who'd been working in Chongjin the whole time, showed up at our place looking gaunt. We heard him whispering in a low voice to our parents in the opposite room, when he burst suddenly into tears.

'Just how badly did you mess up, that now there's a deficit?!' Father yelled, his voice so angry that it nearly covered up the sound of our uncle's bawling.

'Let me guess,' Mother said sharply. 'You've been gambling again?'

'No, I swear. A company in China wanted octopus and promised to pay us back later with soybeans and cornmeal. I told the fishery co-op to send it, but it's been three months and the company hasn't paid us back. So now the co-op is demanding that I pay for it out of my own pocket. I've tried calling, but no one answers. Maybe the company went under. Damn it all.'

'You better go talk to Xiaolong,' Mother said.

Our uncle blew his nose.

'He's got enough problems of his own. We need to have people working in order to have something to sell.'

Father sighed. 'That's true … We were also unable to fill our orders last time. We need to extract more iron ore and sell that to buy some corn.'

As rations were cut and wages came to a stop, miners began to quit and wander around in search of food instead. Countless factories all over the country, both big and small, shut their doors. That night, our uncle snuck across the Tumen River. Neither Mother nor Father could stop him. He told them he would go to Yanji himself to find out what had happened to the company. If he couldn't pay back the fishery cooperative, he would be punished severely and sent to prison. As times had grown tough, anyone who hurt the country's prosperity was subject to even harsher punishment.

Our mother's brother never came back, after crossing the river that day. That was probably the winter of 1994, so I would have been eleven years old.

THREE

My family and I had no idea what was happening in the outside world, but we were able to guess what shape other parts of the country were in from looking at the changes around us. At school, the classrooms weren't even half-full. Our homeroom teacher was nowhere to be seen, and the number of teachers who did stick around dropped to just four or five within a few months.

One day, I was at the Tumen River with Mi when we saw something drifting downstream. It was the body of a woman, floating face-down, with a baby on her back. Mother and child had died together. Had this been ordinary times, my sister and I would have shrieked in shock and run to get someone, but instead we held our breath and watched in silence. The long ties that held the baby sling in place had come undone and were trailing behind the bodies, swaying limply in the current. Later, many more bodies would float past. When they touched the opposite shore, villagers on the Chinese side would push them away with long poles, and, on our side, soldiers and other strong young men would stand watch and shove the bodies into the middle of the river.

One evening, my sisters and I heard our company-housing neighbours chattering loudly outside. Soldiers were dragging a handcart down the main street. The cart was covered in burlap grain sacks, so we couldn't tell at first what was in it — but when we saw several pairs of feet poking out, we knew they were bodies. Usually, if someone died in the night, the neighbours would report it and take care of the body, but after that summer the bodies were left in place. Whenever you passed an empty house, the rotting smell, as if someone was brewing soy sauce, was overwhelming.

Our family managed to get by. Father must have been wise enough to see what was coming. During his deals with Uncle Salamander, he would keep some of the sea cucumber or dried octopus that was delivered to the port and trade it for grain, which he'd been stockpiling. He'd lined his own pockets, as it were. One night, I was awakened by the sound of low voices and the front door opening and closing. Our parents were up to something — they kept walking in and out and grumbling like they were carrying something heavy. I tiptoed quietly to the bedroom door and peeked out. Mother and Father were holding each end of a large sack of grain and carrying it somewhere. Later, my sisters and I figured out that they'd been using a shed behind the house, where we stored farm tools and other odds and ends, as a hiding place. They'd cleared out the shed, pulled up the wooden floorboards and dug a hole in the earth, which they lined with vinyl, to hide the grain. The shed was my mother's first stop every morning — she would head out there with a cooking pot in hand before she started preparing food. When we had all caught on, Mother and

Grandmother sat us down and lectured us at length.

'Now pay attention, all of you,' Grandmother said. 'The Republic can't look after every single one of its subjects anymore. Why do you think they're calling it the "Arduous March"? The only thing in this world you can rely on is your own family. Don't forget that.'

'Listen to your grandmother. Don't mention to *anyone* that we have food to eat. They say half of the houses in the village down the way are empty.'

As we couldn't have others seeing smoke from a cooking fire several times a day, Mother only made rice in the mornings when she lit the stove to heat the house, and we would eat half and save the rest for later. Fortunately, as our father was vice chairman in charge of customs and trade in the city, we had some coal briquettes left in storage and were able to heat the stove even in the middle of the rainy season. The chairman's family, who lived across from us, had also been able to stockpile food, thanks to our father's acumen.

'If we'd stayed in Chongjin, we'd be starving by now,' our mother would say while clearing away dishes. Then her thoughts would turn to Jin, who'd gotten married, and Sun, who was in the army. '*Aigo*, Jin's pregnant now. I wonder how she's getting enough to eat. But Sun must be eating well if she's in the army?'

One day, Chilsung disappeared and had not returned home by sunset. Grandmother saw me pacing outside the stone wall and came out to talk to me.

'Don't worry, Chilsung is fine. I'm sure he'll be home soon. Don't tell your father, and don't let him off the leash next time.'

I squatted down in the corner of the wall. Then I closed my eyes tight and pictured Chilsung. The darkness behind my eyelids slowly paled into a milky light. I saw a road, a field, rows of cornstalks flattened in the wind, and among them, a white creature. Our little Chilsung was lying on his side with his legs stretched out. I opened my eyes wide.

'Grandma! I know where he is. He's in the middle of a cornfield way over there.' I took off running without a thought as to any danger. Grandmother followed me, first trotting, then slowing to a walk. The fields were blanketed in fog.

'Slow down, girl! I told you, Chilsung is fine.'

I passed the train station, crossed the rail crossing, and ran up a low hill. I could see the cornfield. I could hear the cornstalks and the long, flat leaves stirring in the wind. I cupped my hands around my mouth and shouted into the dark.

'Chilsung-*ah*! Chilsung-*ah*!'

Grandmother panted as she climbed over the hill. I stood there with my ears perked, trying to make out any other sounds among the rustling of the leaves. To my right, I heard something that sounded like a short grunt. I pushed my way into the centre of the field and spotted Chilsung's white fur and outstretched legs. When I cradled his head, he yelped and shook my hands off.

'He must be hurt. Don't touch him,' Grandmother said.

'How are we going to get him home?'

'I'll bring your sisters back with the wheelbarrow we keep in the shed. You stay here.'

She disappeared into the dark, and it was just Chilsung and me in the middle of the cornfield.

Bari-ya!

Startled, I looked behind me.

I almost died! Strange men grabbed me and dragged me into the mountains!

Chilsung's breath was weak and shallow. From that moment on, I was not only able to convey my unspoken thoughts but also to hear Chilsung's thoughts, the same way I could hear Sook's. I closed my eyes and thought: *It's alright. I'll keep you safe. You'll be better in no time.*

Mi and our grandmother came back with the wheelbarrow, and we carried Chilsung home in it. When we got to the house, we took a closer look at his injuries: his ear was torn, he had a large open wound on his back and a telephone wire was wrapped around his throat, digging deep into the flesh under his jaw.

Grandmother clucked her tongue. 'Guess he got away from the bastards who were planning to eat him.'

'He's family to us, but meat to everyone else,' Father said. He used a pair of pliers to remove the wire noose and applied ointment to the torn ear and the cut on Chilsung's back. Then he wrapped the injuries with strips of fabric. We took apart the doghouse that Hindungi had lived in back in Chongjin and used the wood for kindling, and spread straw on the floor of the shed to make a bed for Chilsung. It took over two weeks for him to return to full health.

—

All summer, rain fell like a hole had been torn in the sky. The heavy rains that had started at the end of July kept going long past mid-August. The corn and vegetable gardens planted on the mountain slopes were swept away, and even the terraced fields carved high up into the curve of the mountain ridges had collapsed in places from landslides — the red earth beneath the topsoil exposed — or were buried completely under mud. The Tumen River overflowed its banks, and every low place in the city of Musan was puddled with mud. Roads and train tracks buckled and caved. On the radio they said the entire country was underwater. Bodies floated in the flooded fields and at the edges of the cities.

The part of the city we lived in was on relatively high ground, so other than a little bit of flooding on the road to the customs office, we were unaffected. It wasn't until the end of August, nearly ten days after the floodwaters had drained away, that equipment arrived from the city, and soldiers on border patrol and young men who'd survived the famine and flooding were able to repair the railroad tracks and the roads. Though autumn was on its way, there was nothing, not a single crop, left in the fields to harvest. Like us, those who survived were probably nibbling away, bit by bit, at the grain they'd secretly stashed. We had one meal of porridge that was both breakfast and lunch made from boiling roughly ground corn meal with wild greens — groundsel, goosefoot, Chinese plantain, and such — that my sisters and grandmother picked in the fields, and we had rice only at dinner. Hyun, who had a delicate constitution, used to set her spoon down weakly next to her bowl of porridge, and whine:

'Mom, can't we have rice instead? I can't eat this. It's too bitter.'

'Don't be so fussy. A lot of people have died because all they have to eat are wild greens. We just need to make it through the winter.'

After the heat had broken and the crickets were starting to sing, we heard the rumbling of an engine outside. No one, not even anyone from the army base or the People's Committee, had been able to drive one of the Sungri trucks or Soviet-made jeeps for a long time, on account of the fuel shortage, so we stared at each other wide-eyed, wondering if it wasn't perhaps a car from China carrying familiar merchants. Mi took the lead as we headed out to the courtyard. A white car was already making its way up the hill. With my keen eyes, I recognised Uncle Salamander in the front seat. Ah, Grandmother was right! He was indeed a god come down from Heaven. The moment the car pulled up in front of the house, he got out and looked around at us.

'You're all still alive!' he exclaimed.

'*Aigo!* Look who's here! Our saviour!' Grandmother shouted and clasped Uncle Salamander's hands.

Mother came running out of the house, and Father, for once unmindful of looking dignified, bounded into the courtyard in his bare feet.

'Xiaolong is back!'

'Elder Brother, I've been worried sick about you. But things will be better now ... Look back there. There's a shipment of food coming through customs.'

The first thing he unpacked when he got inside was a box of moon cakes for us kids to eat, followed by a sack of rice, three bags of cornmeal, two cans of cooking oil, and some wheat flour. Before anyone could even tell us to help

47

ourselves, we'd ripped open the box, torn off the plastic wrappers, and started munching away, a moon cake in each hand. The sweet filling melted on our tongues. (Years later, after I came to live in London, I would often find myself biting into a slice of pie fresh out of the oven, only to realise that nothing in the world would ever taste quite as good as those moon cakes did that day.) Mother and Grandmother sat with their backs turned to wipe away their tears discreetly, and even Uncle Salamander looked away and took a long drag on his cigarette.

'When the country goes wrong, the little ones are the first to suffer,' he sighed. Then he mentioned his long-awaited business plans to Father. 'China seems to think that the situation here has become very serious. A message came down from the authorities to the merchants' association we've been trading with. It said to deliver food relief immediately, and aid will be provided afterward in the form of loans. Those who can do need to get back to work.'

'But half our workers are gone. Most of the miners have left.'

'There's a company that wants to haul away all that sand and dirt piled up in front of the Tumen River mines and refine it for iron ore. They'll give you money or food, whatever you need, in exchange for it.'

'That's just slag. How much iron do they expect to get?'

'If you're just going to discard it anyway, why not get something for it?'

Our throats were dry from eating the moon cakes, so we took a break to drink some water and rest, and then we started eating again, all the while listening to the grown-ups talk. It was difficult to follow, but we caught the gist of it: there was hope.

'Fine,' Father said. 'Let's go talk it over with our comrade, the chairman.'

Uncle Salamander cleared his throat, took a glance around, and then spoke in a lower voice: 'By the way, Elder Brother ... Have you heard about your wife's brother?'

'Last I saw of him,' Father said, eyeing our mother, 'he was blubbering about being in the red.'

Mother scooted closer. 'Have you heard from him?' she asked.

Uncle Salamander's round eyes grew even wider, and his voice got very quiet. 'Seems he ... fled to the South. Apparently there was a commotion in Shenyang. A group of refugees stormed the embassy.'

'Oh no!'

'How could that be? No one's said anything around here.'

Uncle Salamander looked annoyed by the naivety of his question. 'You know the government is too busy to keep track right now. Between the flooding and the famine, people are dying all over this country. When someone goes missing, it's usually assumed that they died while searching for food.'

Father looked up at the ceiling, half-worried and half-resentful, and then muttered weakly: 'I knew that son of a bitch would ruin this family.'

'Elder Brother, I beg of you, don't breathe a word of this to anyone else. If the Party finds out, we'll deal with it then ... Survival is like a cockfight: you have to anticipate what your opponent is going to do before he does it, so you can get out of the way. Remember that.'

'You're right. *Aigo,* that crazy son of a bitch!'

—

With the start of autumn, starving people descended upon the banks of the Tumen River in droves. Those who had relatives in China crossed over in search of food and money; survivors who'd lost loved ones surged across the border along with workers from factories that had shut down, vowing to bring back money and save their families. No one dared to cross the river in daylight, but once night came they formed groups and crossed the shallow Tumen together. There were fewer than half the number of border guards required to patrol the entire waterway, and the ones who were there were just as hungry as everyone else. They usually pretended not to see the money and goods clutched in the hands of those coming and going across the river. It wasn't until a few years after the famine had subsided that the border patrol was beefed up, and anyone caught trying to cross was punished. But when it began, the Korean-Chinese and Han Chinese living in villages near the Tumen took pity on the refugees and tried to help by giving them food. They would even cook fresh rice to feed those on the verge of starvation who came right to their doors to beg. We still had no idea what was happening to people living in the interior, blocked by wall after wall of mountains. All we heard were rumours — told on the sly by Party workers from the trade bureau who dropped by our house now and then on official business — that the entire Republic was on the verge of mass starvation.

Uncle Salamander returned and started overseeing the haulage of leftover ore, and cargo trucks filled with food arrived. Musan slowly returned to life. The number of workers from other parts of the country also grew. The food situation improved greatly, but most of what came in was taken away by train to Chongjin. Then, one day, right around lunchtime, we had all gathered at home and were just about to enjoy a pot of *sujebi* soup made with dough flakes from the wheat flour we'd received, plus big chunks of potato that we'd sliced up, when we heard someone clearing his throat in the courtyard outside. We looked up to see two men's heads peeking over the windowsill at us. Grandmother nearly dropped her spoon in surprise.

'Who are they? What do they want?' she said.

Their heads lowered back into the courtyard. Father took a look around and then called to them from the windowsill.

'How can I help you, Comrades?'

I heard one of the men say: 'We're from Chongjin. You're the vice chairman, correct?'

'Yes, that's correct.'

'You need to come with us. Please step outside.'

Father went outside without stopping to respond to the wide-eyed, searching look Mother gave him. We all crowded around the window and watched our father's strong, hunched-over back retreating from us with the two men. One of the men wore a grey, short-sleeved Mao suit and carried some kind of ledger behind his back. The outfit, along with the square flag pin, showed that he held a high position. The other man wore a worker's cap and serge jacket like the Great Leader's.

Late that night Father returned home, exhausted. We were sitting around in gloomy silence, not having had the heart to eat dinner, but we poured out onto the wooden veranda upon his arrival. Of course Mother didn't dare ask him what happened. Not even Grandmother could bring herself to ask.

He glanced around at us and asked weakly: 'They eat?'

'How could anyone eat at a time like this? Tell us what happened,' Mother said. Father sank to the ground.

'Let's eat,' he said.

Grandmother couldn't wait any longer either and asked: '*Ya*, who were they?'

'They said they're from the Ministry of State Security. I figured they'd show up sooner or later.'

Even as children, we all knew what that meant. We silently wolfed down our dinner of hard-cooked cornmeal. As soon as the dinner tray was cleared away, Grandmother confronted Father again.

'Out with it already. This was because of their uncle, wasn't it?'

'Yes. Charges were raised against him for causing a deficit and then taking off. I swore I knew nothing about it. Because I really don't.'

'What'll happen,' Mother whispered, 'if rumours get out that he ran to the South?'

'Hush! What are you talking about? That rascal went searching for food and died in the streets.'

'So, then, it's over?'

Father stopped replying. That night, neither of our parents seemed to get much sleep: we could hear them murmuring in their room until late into the night, sometimes raising their voices at each other. We tossed and turned, and Grandmother didn't get much sleep either because she kept tucking the blankets back around us and whispering to us to go to sleep. The next morning Father left for Chongjin with the two men.

This was the start of the misfortune that visited our family.

Three days passed, and then five, and still Father didn't return home. Mother went to the train station every day to wait for him. Then one day, a group of soldiers and a familiar-looking Party official came banging on our door. The official handed our mother a slip of paper.

'You've been issued a summons,' he said.

'What does this mean?'

'You must vacate. New tenants are arriving. Report to the district office right away.'

Mother left at once for the office, which wasn't far from where we lived. The soldiers came into the house without bothering to remove their boots and began opening all of the doors. They started carrying out the refrigerator and television set. Grandmother tried to stop them.

'What are you doing? You think you can just take other people's things?!'

'Out of the way.'

The Party official tried to pacify her: 'Ma'am, there's no point arguing with us. Now that you've received a summons, your property is being seized, and you're being relocated.'

Later I learned that Mother and Mi, who'd finished secondary school, and Jung and Sook, who were still in school, were told to go to Puryong, where they would be assigned jobs. So what was to become of Grandmother, Hyun, and me? No slips of paper came our way; our names weren't even mentioned. I don't know how the days and hours passed after that. We spent that first night clinging to each other on the floor of our emptied room, clothes and blankets strewn all around us. When we awoke the next morning, Mi was gone. Our mother seemed completely unruffled by it.

'That sly girl … She kept saying she was going to cross the river one day and flee to China. Well, she's all grown up now, so she'll make it on her own, wherever she is.'

Mother kept trying to reassure Grandmother: she'd asked the chairman to keep an eye on them; Father would only be gone for another month, two at the latest; he'd done so much for the country that, of course, this was all just a minor misunderstanding. She also made a point of adding that Grandmother would be assigned to a collective farm, so she would receive food rations in exchange for helping out there. But no one knew better than Mother herself that this was all just talk.

The day my mother and sisters left I stood off to the side and refused to cry. They each carried a small bundle of rations. As they walked away, they kept glancing back. They were looking at us, of course, but they were probably also engraving the image of our beloved home in their minds. None of us knew it was the last time we would ever see each other. At some point they started showing up in my dreams. They stand beside each other, Mother, Sook, and Jung, looking at me from a distance, smiling gently and not saying a word. Perhaps these are their ghosts.

Grandmother decided it was best for us to stay put until the new tenants arrived, just in case Father returned in the meantime. Unable to turn on the lights, we were eating some boiled potatoes for our dinner when we heard footsteps outside. Then we heard someone clear his throat and mutter, as if to himself: 'I wonder if anyone's home?'

Hyun recognised Uncle Salamander's voice and called out: 'Uncle! We're here!' Grandmother rushed out to greet him. She fell to the ground and clung to his legs.

'*Aigo!* Our family is ruined!'

'Grandmother, please stand up. I heard what happened.'

He lit a cigarette and let out a deep sigh. Grandmother filled him in on everything that had transpired, punctuating the story with complaints.

'I should've gotten here sooner!' he said. He paced back and forth, deep in thought, and then turned to Grandmother. 'Pack your things. And dress the kids in warm layers.'

'Are we going somewhere? It's the middle of the night …'

'Let's cross the river. We'll figure out a way for you to survive once we're there.'

'But what about the others?'

'Elder Brother's a resourceful man. I have no doubt he'll be back, so I'm taking you across the river to wait for him there. When he returns we'll get the others back from Puryong too.'

Grandmother had no reason not to go along with his plan. To her as well, Uncle Salamander must have seemed our only hope. The moment he'd arrived we were happier

55

and more reassured to see him than if it had been Father. Grandmother went into the shed, pulled up the floorboards, scooped out all of the grain that our mother had saved for us when she left and filled three large sacks, one for each of us. Uncle Salamander lifted Hyun's sack and mine in one hand like they weighed nothing.

We stayed off the main roads and travelled along a wooded path toward the riverbank. Chilsung followed close behind. Uncle Salamander knew, as well as the rest of us, the location of every guard post and the places where the river was narrow and shallow. We headed upstream and chose a spot where the Tumen swept, in a big semi-circle, around a large patch of gravel. It was where my sisters and I used to go in the winter to play on the ice. The water was cold, but Uncle Salamander tucked my sister and me under his arms to help us across. Grandmother slipped and fell twice.

Our little group made it to the other side, onto Chinese soil. The cold air barrelling down from the slope of the mountains seemed to penetrate our clothes. We walked late into the night, for over thirty *li*, and arrived at a small village outside of Chongshan. We could see a few lights in the darkness.

'Stay here and take care of your grandmother,' Uncle Salamander said. 'I'll go check it out first.'

He warned Grandmother to stay away from the main road, and instructed her to wait for him in the forest. After a long while, he returned and took us to a farmhouse just past an orchard where a farmer, his mother, his wife, and their daughter (who was the same age as our sister Jung) all lived. We felt much better once we were resting on their warm, heated floor. The house was divided into two rooms, but one was occupied by the husband and wife. The farmer kept calling Uncle Salamander 'Elder Brother,' so we figured they were close; later we learned that, before he was married, the farmer had worked in a restaurant next to Uncle Salamander's office.

Grandmother, Hyun, and I offered to sleep in the small shed they kept at the end of the orchard. It was filled with fruit boxes, farm tools, wheelbarrows, and other things, but Uncle Salamander and the farmer shoved all of it over to one side and covered the floor with plastic sheeting and a blanket to make it more comfortable for us.

'Elder Brother will come to join you in no time,' Uncle Salamander reassured us. 'I'll give instructions to a friend in Musan that I trust, so don't worry. In the meantime, I'll look for Mi, as you said she's already on this side of the river. I hope she hasn't run into any problems.'

With that, he left. The farmer's daughter was delighted by Chilsung. She wrapped her arms around his neck and hugged him for so long that I started to feel jealous. The rest of her family must have felt it was good to have a dog around, as wild boars and rabbits would come down from the nearby mountains and damage the crops. The next morning the family was already making a racket and calling the dog by name the same way we did: 'Chilsung-*ah*! Chilsung-*ah*!'

—

We scraped through the rest of that autumn by stretching the grain we'd brought and the *renminbi* currency that

Uncle Salamander had slipped into our hands before he left. We were also given some rice as payment for helping the family to bring in their harvest.

One evening, when the first snow had fallen, an ethnic Korean farmer from a neighbouring village dropped by. He told us that a North Korean man had showed up at his house with the name and address of the orchard owner written down. Our grandmother burst into tears and clapped her hands.

'*Aigo!* That has to be my son!'

It was dark by then, so the farmer got up early the next morning and went alone to the other village. How can I possibly describe the thrill of seeing my father's familiar, lanky slouch appear on the path between the snow-laden branches of the orchard? Grandmother, Hyun, and I raced over in a knot to greet him. He was much thinner than the last time we'd seen him, and he reminded me of an old lattice door — as though he might break in half and fall over at any moment. He let out a strange sound, something halfway between a laugh and a groan. His shoulders drooped, and he wore a padded winter army coat with the cotton batting sticking out here and there. The soles of his shoes flapped open like a dog's tongue. Grandmother went outside to our little kitchen, which was just a wooden box set up in the corner of the shed with a bit of roof for cover, and came back with rice, salted vegetables, and some *dwenjang* soybean-paste soup boiled with sliced potatoes. Ah, it had been so long since we'd all sat down to breakfast together! Though he was the only one who'd returned to us, we felt like we finally had our family back. He would take care of us and keep us safe.

'Rice!' Father exclaimed in wonder, digging his spoon into the metal bowl.

'We get to eat rice everyday here,' I bragged.

Grandmother, Hyun, and I were surprised by what he did next. Without any word or gesture to us to go ahead and start eating, he picked up the pot of soup that we were all supposed to eat from, poured over half of it onto his own rice and started shovelling the food into his mouth. He had his face down close to the bowl. We could see the top of his head: the hair had fallen out, leaving sparse clumps, and the grey had turned nearly all white. Grandmother turned to us as we sat and stared at him, our spoons motionless in our hands.

'You two, go on now. Let's eat.'

I could tell that Father had changed. He'd never been much of a talker, but Grandmother murmured to us later, with damp eyes, that his experiences in the labour camp had changed him. He slept like the dead. Night and day, he lay curled up in the innermost corner of the shed, sleeping until the next mealtime, when he would slowly rise, eat some more, and fall back to sleep. After about two weeks of this, he finally seemed to come to. He started hanging around outside the shed, and would go out to the orchard in search of firewood to help Grandmother with the cooking. Once we went with him across the main road to the edge of the forest, where we could see the Tumen River. He stared for a long time at the mountains stripped bare on the other side and at the houses clustered along the edges of the fields like grey mushrooms.

'Sons of bitches!'

With that, he turned and stalked back to the orchard. We lingered there a moment longer, studying the North Korean side of the river visible through the tree branches. There was no sign of anyone in the fields or along the foot of the mountains. To whom had his curses been aimed?

Toward the end of the year, when the ice was frozen solid and the distant mountains were covered in snow, Chilsung began barking more and more at night. Whether because of their daughter's badgering or because of the animals that sometimes came down from the hills, the farmer's wife had asked Grandmother to let them keep Chilsung in their front yard, in a doghouse they built from some cement blocks. I'm sure he would have preferred to live with us, but he was kept tied there and couldn't do anything about it. We didn't feel too sad about it. Anytime we wanted to see him we only had to cross the orchard and head toward the courtyard of the farmhouse; Chilsung would welcome us with his ears pressed back, his tail wagging. 'Lately he's been barking like crazy,' the farmer's daughter told us. 'It's keeping us awake at night.'

'North Koreans who crossed the river have been going around in packs and stealing grain and preserves,' the farmer's mother explained.

Hyun and I slept so soundly every night that we could have been carried off by *dokkaebi* and been none the wiser, but our grandmother seemed to know what was happening.

'I saw them too,' she said. 'A whole family spent a couple of days hiding in the forest: the woman had a baby on her back, and they both had a kid in each hand. I've also heard people walking around outside at night.'

Stories of starving North Koreans wandering across the border in search of food were by no means uncommon in villages near the river, but, one day, rumours spread that a family had been murdered in Nanping. People had been finding bodies in their sheds and in the forest — North Koreans who'd frozen to death or died of exhaustion — but this was the first instance of a Chinese family being killed. It happened in a remote house in a village on the Chinese side of the border. The police began scouring the surrounding forests and questioning people. Even Koreans who'd come across earlier and had settled with relatives were arrested in droves and sent back across the river. Others took it upon themselves to return, frightened by the brutal change of mood.

In the past, Chinese and North Koreans living along the Tumen (which they'd once regarded as nothing more than a village stream) would cross back and forth to visit each other and even exchange crops, but once the famine started in the North, the crackdowns began. The farmer we were staying with told us that if the Chinese police found us there, he and his family would be punished too, and that although they felt bad for us, we would have to go. He suggested we build a temporary shelter out of sight in the mountains, and offered to pay us with food in exchange for working in his orchard. Father went with the farmer into the mountains behind the village to find a place where we could hide; the following morning, he packed up our things and took the three of us up into the woods. He'd found some level ground on a low slope covered in underbrush where a steeply-sided ravine died out; the water flowing down the ravine had pooled next to the clearing and frozen in place.

Father and the farmer used a pickaxe and shovel to break the frozen ground. They dug down until the sides reached over my head, just as if they were digging a hole to bury a *kimchi* jar, and cut branches from nearby trees to weave a conical roof, which was lashed in place to a wooden post erected at the centre of the dugout. The branches were then lined with ripped-up fertiliser sacks and covered with thickly needled pine and fir branches to keep out rain and snow. We worked together for several days to make the inside of the dugout hut more comfortable. Father created a traditional heated *ondol* floor for us by lining the bare dirt with wide, flat stones, leaving channels in between and covering it with scraps of vinyl scavenged from the farmer's house. Cardboard boxes were broken down and spread on top. Grandmother, Hyun and I carved out a tiny kitchen space at the entrance to the dugout where we could cook, and stacked rocks to form a rudimentary stove big enough to set a pot or kettle on. When we lit a fire in the stove, the heat and smoke passed under the floor through the channels and escaped out a chimney at the back of the hut. Father had done such a good job with the floor that not a single whiff of smoke snuck into the room.

So much had happened to our family that I was more than happy to sleep snuggled up next to our grandmother while our father snored away, guarding the entrance to our tiny hut with his body. Ah, a home of our own! The only part I was sad about was Chilsung. The farmer had remarked on how fond his daughter was of the dog, and offered to buy him. Father hadn't said a word about it, though I assumed he took the money. But I figured it was better for Chilsung to be raised with love in their house than to starve with us in the mountains.

FOUR

Winter in the foothills of the Baekdu mountain range was beautiful and harsh. The slope we sheltered ourselves against was probably one among the hundreds of baby mountains that flowed down from Mount Baekdu itself. The snow fell for so many days straight that the whole world was a storm of white both night and day. We stayed cooped up in our dugout hut the whole time, like hibernating animals. Snow weighed heavily on the spruce, larch, and pine trees until the branches split down the middle or snapped off of the trunks entirely; during a break in the flurries, when we stuck our heads out from behind the straw mat that served as our door, the ice coating the branches glittered radiantly in the sun. But those icy branches looked more deadly than pretty to me.

Hyun, who was one year older but had been more like a younger sister ever since we were little, died that winter. One night a blizzard began to rage, and the wind whistled sharply.

'Grandma, I'm so cold I can't sleep …'

I kept hearing Hyun's faint voice, muffled by the

blanket. Each time, Grandmother would tuck the blanket more tightly over her head and comfort her.

'There, now. It'll be morning soon. Then it won't be as cold.'

The wind whistling through the trees grew stronger and we heard a groan, like a huge wave bearing down, just before the storm crashed in on us without mercy. Our roof of woven branches flew off. Snow piled up on our blankets and threatened to bury the entire hut. Father sprang up and groped around in the dark for the tree branches and empty fertiliser bags that had served as our roof, but it had all blown away already. He began scooping up snow with his bare hands and tossing it outside, but soon gave up. The snow coming in was much greater than what he could dig out with his hands. When my blanket got so heavy that it was pressing down on my small body and making it hard to breathe, I crawled out and helped Grandmother scoop up the snow with a bowl and our cooking pot. Then I got back under the blanket, rubbed my hands together and tucked them into my armpits to warm them. My teeth chattered.

The snow didn't start to die down until close to dawn, and finally stopped completely when the sun rose. Our beloved hut was in a gruesome state. The storm had passed, but the wind was still strong enough to turn the snow that had accumulated on the tree branches into a fine, white powder that hung in the air. Father ran around cutting branches while Grandmother and I collected them and dragged them back to the hut. We were able to do some makeshift repairs.

When the roof flew off again a few days later, Father

despaired. He could have taken more of the vinyl sheeting the farmer would need in the spring to rebuild his greenhouses and used it to build us a roof strong enough to last for years — but he would sooner have taken us back to the farmer's house and begged him to let us move back in. Father said generosity was like cooked rice: the longer it sat out, the faster it spoiled. In other words, if you kept imposing on people, then when you really needed their help later they would turn their backs on you. Grandmother nodded.

That day, the three of us were so busy clearing away the snow, shaking out the blankets and rebuilding the roof that we forgot all about Hyun. Father tied branches together with plastic twine to form a frame and wove leafy branches into it, while Grandmother dug out the dry branches and twigs for kindling that had been stacked beside the entrance to the hut, shook out all of the snow and used the wood to get the fire restarted. The smell of the wood burning made me feel warmer already. When we were sitting inside the hut, our breath white in the air, Grandmother finally realised that Hyun was gone.

'Where did little Hyun go?' she asked.

She checked under all the blankets, and Father groped around every corner of the hut. We went outside. Father searched all around and found Hyun in a thickly wooded area filled with large trees. She was lying on her side, curled up tight like a dried anchovy. Father picked her up and Grandmother stayed by their side, shaking her head.

'Wake up, child!' she said.

Hyun stayed curled up as though frozen in place. We brought her into the hut, placed her under the blanket, and rubbed her hands, feet, and legs. She opened her eyes and stared at us as if she'd just woken from a long sleep.

'What were you doing out there in the cold?' Grandmother asked.

'I had to pee …'

'You should've come back right away. You almost froze to death!'

Hyun closed her eyes and didn't respond. She looked like she was sleeping. Father kept rubbing her hands and feet.

'Mother,' he said urgently, 'she's not warming up. Heat up some water and feed it to her.'

Grandmother went outside, filled the cooking pot with snow, and boiled it on the stove. Then she filled a small bowl with warm water and held it up to Hyun's mouth, but Hyun only sipped enough to wet her tongue a little and went limp again. We unpacked our belongings and pulled out all the clothes — which were frozen stiff — and squeezed, rubbed, and sat on them until they were filled with our body heat. Then we piled them on top of Hyun and wrapped the blanket around her. The fire had built up nicely. The cardboard that covered the floor stones was starting to warm up. But a very soft, smoke-like *something* hovered darkly over Hyun's body. I didn't know what it was, but I was afraid to get any closer or to try to make it go away.

Hey, Big Sister, I thought to her, *I know you're trying to leave us*.

We tucked our legs under the blanket and dozed off where we sat. Sometime in the night, Hyun passed. She'd grown too weak, and couldn't bear the cold. But none of us — not Father, Grandmother, or I — shed a single tear.

Father wrapped her small body in several layers of clothes and fertiliser sacks. As he left the hut with Hyun, he narrowed his eyes at us.

'Don't follow me!'

—

Winter passed, and bright green shoots poked up through the gaps in the lingering snow. Grandmother and I went down the mountain to pick the greens that had just begun to grow along the edges of the fields and the ridges of the paddies that had not yet been ploughed up. All we had was some salt and a little *dwenjang* that the farmer's family had given us, but when we boiled the greens and seasoned them with the *dwenjang* or made them into a soup, the fragrant scent of the greens complemented the deep flavour of the fermented bean paste, and made for a perfect meal with a bowl of rice. And of course that was white rice we were enjoying!

Father did some work for the farmer's family and returned with a sack of wheat flour — not the earthy, brown flour we were used to, but a strange variety that was as white as snow. Grandmother ground up mugwort shoots and added it to the flour to make dough, and then roughly moulded the dough into small, flat *gaetteok* cakes and steamed them.

One morning Father put on a thick, padded coat over his faded Mao suit, just as he used to do before heading off to work; he tightened the laces of his shoes and left home. I knew instinctively that he was heading out on a long journey. He stroked my head for a moment and then quickly pulled his hand away and coughed dryly.

'Bari,' he said, 'I'll be back in a few days. Take care of your grandmother.'

'Where are you going?'

He didn't answer me, and turned to Grandmother instead.

'Mother, it'll take about five days. There's plenty of food. Should last you at least two months, so don't starve yourself. Eat as much as you want.'

Grandmother and I stood there in silence as he left. I wanted to follow him down the mountain and all the way to the road through the orchard, but I knew he would only narrow his eyes at me and say: 'Aren't you too old for this?' So I stayed by Grandmother's side. Father quickly disappeared amongst the trees. Grandmother must've seen that I was feeling down and wanted to distract me. She patted me gently on the back and whispered: 'Bari, look over beneath that tree. Pheasants!'

Indeed, a male pheasant with golden feathers, a blue band around his neck, and a proud tail sticking straight up was cocking his head this way and that, while a female with a round, grey belly was foraging through the dry underbrush in search of something to eat. It never fails that, once someone is out of sight, your thoughts of that person leave with them. It felt like ages had already passed since Father had spent the winter with us. Just as I now only saw my mother and two sisters who'd left for Puryong in my dreams, my father's leaving was like a spot in the sky where a cloud had just passed.

On nights after we'd steamed potatoes and cooked

rice and finished our dinner, and owls were hooting in the woods, I would plead with Grandmother to tell me stories. Listening to her old tales made me feel like I was back in that house with the wide courtyard at the top of the hill in Chongjin. My sisters would be playing cat's-cradle or a clapping game in the room on the other side of the house, and any moment now our mother would come out of the kitchen with a basket of *gaetteok* that she'd steamed in the cauldron or *sulppang* leavened with alcohol, and I would hear her call out merrily: 'Girls, come have some snacks!' I could hear my sisters laughing in delight as they thumped across the floor.

'Did you hear what I said, child?' Grandmother asked me.

'No … the last thing I heard you say was that Princess Bari was the seventh daughter.'

'That's right. The six older daughters appear one after the other and burst into tears: "Our poor mother! Our poor father!" The queen turns to them and says: "Alas, another girl! Your father, His Majesty the King, will collapse from anger, so go to the stonemason and ask him to carve us a stone chest. Place the baby inside of it. Then tiptoe all the way to the Dragon Swamp, slowly, slowly, and toss it in!" But those foolish girls take off running, the heavy stone chest hoisted onto their shoulders, their backs, their heads. They keep pace by chanting, *Uh-gi yung-cha! Uh-gi yung-cha!* When they reach the swamp, a flute plays. It is the voice of Heaven. Sky and Earth stick together, blocking their way. They call out: "O Heavenly Lord! If you mean to kill us, then kill us. If you mean to strike us down, then strike us down. We've done nothing wrong. We are at the service of the king and are doing his bidding." Heaven and Earth split apart again. They toss the chest into the swamp and say: "Ah, now we can never again return to the palace."'

'Grandma, I thought you said she was abandoned in a forest, like me.'

'Sometimes it's a forest. Other times it's a river, or the sea. Sometimes she's saved by a crane, and other times by a magpie. Sometimes, a golden tortoise appears and saves her.'

'And after that she's raised by an elderly hermit couple?'

'Well, sometimes she's rescued by the Dragon King in his underwater palace. Then, after she's all grown up, the king and queen become very ill, and all their subjects fall ill too. What's to be done? A fortune teller is consulted, and they're told that the only way they'll be saved is if the seventh daughter they abandoned, Princess Bari, returns. A girl is brought forth from the mountains, but they're not sure that it's her and not some evil spirit or ghost impostor. The girl takes a few tiny steps forward and says: 'Mother, there's proof.'

'What proof?' the queen asks.

'The blood on the door is still wet from when you pricked my ring finger as a baby and left a mark. I'll prick my finger again, and we'll see if the blood matches.'

'The queen agrees, so the girl pricks her ring finger, wincing from the pain, and adds a drop to the blood on the papered door. Sure enough, it congeals together, proving it is the same blood. The queen exclaims: "*Aigo!* You've grown up as bright as the full moon and as strong as the king of the beasts! Was it the water? Was it the sunshine? Was it the dew? How did you grow up so well?"'

'I know what happens next! She has to bring back the life-giving water to save her parents and the people of the world, right?'

'Clever little Bari! I told you the story once, and you remembered the whole thing. So they tell her, if you go to where the sun sets over there in the western sky, all the way to the ends of the Earth, you'll find the life-giving water. While Bari journeys through the ailing country, across the ocean and over the mountains, she is helped by gods and spirits — but she also has to wash other people's clothes and weed their fields and do all sorts of lowly tasks. She repels ghosts and travels to Hell. She saves the sinners who are trapped there, and when she reaches the western sky, there is a guardian totem pole there, a *jangseung*, waiting for her. Bari loses a bet with the totem pole and has to marry him and have his children and work for him for nine long years before he will give her the life-giving water. She endures all manner of hardship there at the ends of the Earth, and on her journey back she sees the boats that travel to the other world. And on the decks of those boats are souls burdened with their karma.'

'Grandma, you left out the part about how she gets the life-giving water!'

'Yes, yes, you're right. Granny forgot. Bari asks the *jangseung* for the water, and that rat tells her: "You've had it all along. It's the same water we use every day to cook rice and do laundry."'

'So Princess Bari did all that work for nothing?'

'No, no. She gained the ability to recognise which water

gives you eternal life.'

'What does that mean?'

'You'll understand when you're older. When she returns and sprays the life-giving water on her parents, they recover and the whole world gets better again. Ever since then, Old Grandmother Bari has lived inside of us. She's inside me and inside you, too.'

I heard the story of Princess Bari many times while lying next to my grandmother in the dark. Back then, I used to dream all kinds of dreams and, as I mentioned before, other than the one in which my mother and two sisters stare at me silently, none of them left much of an impression on me — except a dream I had about the Great Princess Bari. But I don't remember for certain whether I had that dream when I was living in the dugout hut with Grandmother, or after she passed away.

—

There are times when I am in the middle of a dream and I think to myself, *I'm dreaming right now*, even as I keep following the course of the dream. When the Great Princess Bari appeared in my dream, I was strolling along a wide, empty beach. At the other end of the beach, on the white sand devoid of any tree and under the blue sky devoid of any cloud, stood a single house. It had a huge tiled roof and latticed windows and doors. The next thing I knew, I was inside. Pillars with a circumference as wide as my arms could reach around stood in a row. Sunlight slanted down into a broad corridor that looked like a palace or temple that I would later come to visit after I'd left the North for good, but stone walls blocked the light from reaching any further. It was so dark that I didn't move from where I stood, but then the room began to brighten, as if someone had turned on a small lamp, and the faint, glimmering light spread up the walls all the way to the ridgepole at the top of the high ceiling. I took a step forward, and then another step. Someone appeared in the light. It wasn't a golden light, rather a bright glare like the sun on a summer day, and in it hovered the white silhouette of a person. I wasn't sure if it was her hair colour or just the light, but her hair was all white and held in an old-fashioned chignon with a long hairpin, and she wore white mourning clothes. The countless pleats in her long, loose skirt swayed as if stirred by a stray breeze. Her face was white too; I could not tell whether she was old or young, but I could sense that she was smiling gently. The figure, which floated there impassively, vanished when I took a step back and reappeared when I took a step forward. But when I stepped into the room again later, she was gone. I committed the vision to memory. I never saw her again, but that was because Chilsung and my grandmother would sometimes appear in my dreams instead to help me, even after I'd travelled to a faraway country.

Five days passed, and then months passed, and still Father had not returned. Grandmother had told me a few days after he left: 'He's gone to Puryong to bring back the family.' But I'd already known. It was dangerous enough for him to have escaped when he was being punished for our uncle's crimes, but it went without saying that going back there for the rest of the family was just plain stupid. Yet what could we do? Had I been in his shoes, I would've done the same.

When summer began, Grandmother and I started foraging for mushrooms and medicinal herbs deep in the mountains for us to eat with the grain we received from the farmer's family. We would each fill a sack with bellflower and bracken, which grew in abundance, and *lingzhi* mushrooms, which were called the 'mushroom of immortality' and earned us the most money when sold. We also collected *chaga* and *neungi* mushrooms, and a type of medicinal rhubarb, and peonies.

Grandmother knew everything there was to know about the mountains. She taught me how to avoid poisonous mushrooms and plants. If we'd sold the patch of *lingzhi* mushrooms we'd discovered one day in a thicket on the slope of a hill amidst a tangle of oaks and alder, we could have made a fortune. But instead we limited ourselves to a few handfuls now and then, mixed in with the bracken and bellflower roots, in exchange for a steady supply of rice and sundry food items. One day, we filled our sacks with bracken and headed for our treasure trove to collect a few mushrooms. I worked at the top of the slope while Grandmother, who said her legs were bothering her, rested and warmed herself in the sun in a flat clearing at the bottom of the hill. I spotted some astragalus root growing from the stump of a tree, and remembered that Grandmother had told me it was good for restoring energy in the elderly.

'Grandma!' I yelled. 'I've found astragalus!'

I'd called out to where she was sitting with her back turned at the bottom of the hill, but she remained squatting and didn't budge. She had the hoe, so I hopped and slid down the hill to her.

'Grandma, I need the hoe,' I said, and tapped her on the arm. She slumped over to one side. Her arm and shoulder were stiff. When I looked down at her face, her eyes were closed. A single line of blood had trickled out of her nose and pooled in the wrinkles around the sides of her mouth. I placed my head against her chest and listened for a heartbeat, and I even tried placing one finger under her nose to feel for any breath, but there was no question that she was dead.

I sat there for a long while and wept openly. After much time had passed, I felt like my crying had echoed out across the empty forest and was making its way back to me, so I stopped. I sat there blankly for a little longer, and then started to dig away the earth with the hoe. I didn't have the strength to dig very deep; I think I only made it far enough to cover up her body and no more. I dragged her body into the hole and covered her with a thick layer of soil. I couldn't bear to watch her face disappear beneath the dirt, so I took the empty fertiliser sack that we always had with us and used it to cover her face.

'When Father returns,' I told her, 'we'll give you a proper burial in a nice, sunny spot.'

I trudged back down the mountain. Now I was the only one left in our empty hut.

How many days did I lie there alone? One night, I awoke with a start. An owl was hooting somewhere far off, deep in the woods. I didn't know what it was, but something was calling me. It wasn't a voice or anything with form, and yet something like an invisible thread seemed to be tied to one of the hairs on my head and was tugging very gently. The annoying sensation reminded me of walking into a spider web in the dark, but instead of waving my hands around to try to shake it off, I let it happen. I poked my head out of the hut and gazed off at the pale dawn breaking on the horizon.

I got ready to leave. I dressed warmly in layers, and on top of the farmer's daughter's old tracksuit, I put on a blue hooded parka made of some synthetic fabric that was likewise a hand-me-down from the daughter and zipped it up all the way to my chin. Into the canvas rucksack that our family had been using ever since Musan, I added the emergency food supply I'd spent the entire previous day preparing. I'd made *gaetteok* from the flour we had left and wrapped them in plastic, fried the uncooked rice and ground it into a powder and washed the single gourd's worth of small black beans left over from the sprouts my grandmother had grown in a pan and divided into plastic baggies. Of the household items we'd acquired from the family, there were several hard plastic soda bottles. We'd used them to store water, bean paste, and cooking oil. I decided to take only the water bottle.

When I made it down the mountain and was turning the corner into the orchard, I heard the familiar sound of Chilsung's bark. I wanted to see him before I left, so I headed toward the house instead. As soon as I came up to him, tiptoeing quietly so as not to wake the family, Chilsung wagged his tail so hard that his entire butt moved side to side. I wrapped my arms around him.

I'm off to look for Mum and Dad, I said. *Once I find them, we'll all be together again.*

Chilsung's response thundered inside my head.

Bari-ya! Take me with you! I can help! Undo the leash!

No, wait for us here. I'll be back in a few days.

When I was done reasoning with him, I crossed the orchard and headed back through the forest down to the riverside path. The Tumen River was right below where I stood.

I took off my clothes, perched the bundle on top of my head and waded into the water, waving my arms in a semblance of swimming just as I had when I was a child. When I couldn't feel the bottom, I doggy-paddled, and when my feet touched the river bottom again, I walked. I had made it across.

The sunrise was spreading its way down the gently sloping side of Mount Gunham, when I heard the sound of water spraying and splashing right behind me. I turned to look and there was Chilsung, shaking water off his coat. He'd freed himself and followed me right across the river. Instead of scolding him, I untied the broken rope from his neck and tossed it away.

We walked along the foot of the mountain, heading southeast toward the distant fields so we could avoid the village. The mountains on the North Korean side of the river were bare except for green shoots — they'd been stripped clean of trees for firewood, or for planting terraced fields. I didn't know how to get to Puryong, but I'd heard that it was on the way to Chongjin, where I'd grown up. I figured I might find a freight train loaded with ore somewhere along the way. Chilsung and I walked aimlessly under the blazing sun.

—

The next part was like a long dream. Whenever we spotted a passerby, Chilsung and I would quickly hide in the bushes by the side of the road, or behind a rock, and wait for the person to pass. Once, we saw a mother and daughter coming toward us, but we didn't bother to hide. They were so starved and exhausted that they didn't even turn to look at us, let alone say anything. At the top of a hill overlooking a village, we saw the body of a man lying face-up toward the sun. His mouth was agape and his eyes were open; a little foam had seeped out of the corner of his mouth, and his lips and cheeks were dried stiff. A short distance away from the body, I saw his spirit sitting on the branch of a pine tree. He looked like a puff of smoke emerging from a chimney on a cloudy day.

Where ya going? he asked.

To find my parents.

No point in that, he muttered. *They're all dead.*

I didn't respond. His smoke-like ghost hovered over us, muttering: *I'm hungry. Gimme food. Gimme something to eat.* When Chilsung growled and bared his teeth, the man vanished, as if swept away on a breeze.

I decided there wasn't much benefit to travelling during the day, as we had to take long detours each time we came across a village or factory, so I led Chilsung up into the surrounding mountains. It wasn't until we made it to one of the peaks that we spotted railroad tracks winding off in the distance. *Okay,* I thought to myself, *if we follow those tracks, we'll find our way to Puryong.* As I'd made up my mind to sleep during the day and walk only at night, I immediately spread my jacket out on the underbrush and lay down. Chilsung lay pressed up against my side, his chin propped on his paws as he kept watch over me. When I awoke, shivering from the cold, the sky was filled with stars. It looked like all of the lights were on in the houses of some distant world. I nearly reached my hand out to try to pluck the biggest star that seemed to dangle right before my eyes.

I headed down the mountain in the dark toward the railroad tracks that I'd spotted during the day. I felt the crunch of gravel underfoot before I saw the tracks. Chilsung and I stepped over the metal rails and up onto the wooden ties, and followed the tracks all night. I can't remember if we stopped somewhere to sleep or if we walked straight on into the next night, but we eventually arrived near Gomusan Station. The whole area had been abandoned. We were walking down an alley past a long row of empty houses when I had the distinct sensation that there were people inside.

Who's she?

Whispers were carried to me on the wind. Dark shapes as distinct as black clothes hanging on a clothesline in the middle of a moonless night began to appear one after another. One of them brushed past me and suddenly spoke in a clear voice:

Where are you going?

I wasn't afraid. Even when it was just Grandmother and me in the dugout hut, with tigers and lynxes prowling right outside, I hadn't been afraid; nor was I afraid later, when I was on my own in the woods.

80

What's it to you where I'm going? Do you think I'm afraid of you?

The black shapes whispered to each other:

She says she's not afraid!

Chilsung and I walked straight ahead without paying the shapes any attention, and came to a stop in front of a house. It had a wide courtyard and a wooden veranda, just like our house back in Musan, and the gate was open. I was about to go through it when Chilsung dug in his hind legs and let out a low growl.

It's okay, boy. We'll rest here until the sun comes up and then head to the station. When I walked into the courtyard, a breeze blew past me and whirled around the yard. I was about to step up onto the veranda when I heard a hoarse female voice right behind me.

You bad girl. How dare you walk right into someone else's house?

When I turned to look, a woman with dishevelled hair was standing in front of the kitchen door. I could tell that it was the owner of the house — and that it was not a living person. Chilsung growled again.

I'm sorry, Auntie. I was looking for my mother, but I got so tired that I thought I could just rest here a little before I kept going.

Get rid of the dog. It's scaring the kids.

He's my little brother. He won't hurt anyone. Auntie, how did you die?

Quiet giggles erupted in the corner.

She says that dog is her little brother!

Two children were standing side by side in the house.

The taller one was a girl, the shorter one a boy. They looked to be about seven and four. I sat on the veranda while the woman and her two kids stood as far away from me as they could.

We can't leave, the woman said. *We're waiting for their father to come back. He and I went all the way to Hoeryong and Chongjin to look for food, but there were no trains and we had to walk. It took us three days to get home. We found our children frozen and starved to death. I died right then of shock. My husband left and hasn't returned. Look at the yard. Those are our neighbours. They all went first. We were the last to go.*

I looked at the spirits, clumped together and wavering like dark smoke in the courtyard and on the threshold of the gate. I thought of what my grandmother would do and took the *gaetteok* I'd made before leaving from my knapsack, pulled off little pieces, and began tossing them into the courtyard. I tossed some to the woman and her two kids inside the house as well.

Eat up, everyone. Eat, eat, before you go. You have some too, and you, and you.

The shapes vanished at once. I gave a piece to Chilsung and had a small bite for myself before slipping into a deep sleep.

In the morning, we walked to the station. There were no employees, and no sign that anyone had been there in a while. I was squatting outside the station building when an elderly woman came tottering toward me.

'I've never seen you before. What neighbourhood are you from?' she asked.

'I'm from Musan.'

'Why'd you come here then? You should've crossed the river instead. My son and daughter-in-law left the country that way a long time ago. Said they were looking for work.'

'Grandmother, if I need to get to Puryong, should I take a train from here?'

'Train? Do people still take those? The train stopped coming here ages ago. Everyone who was still alive ran off as well. Let's see. I suppose it would only take a day for an adult to reach Puryong on foot.'

The old woman let her basket drop. It held some pine bark and a few scraps of bellflower root.

'This stuff has been keeping me alive. You hurry on home now. Or go to the station at Chongjin like the other urchins. That's the only way to survive, by begging and stealing.'

I reached behind to pull another *gaetteok* from the plastic bag in my knapsack, but the old woman snatched the whole packet from me. I would never have guessed from her slow shuffle and the way she'd spoken that her hands could've moved that fast. She stuffed two of the *gaetteok* in her mouth at once and started to chew. Her molars must have fallen out, because she nibbled futilely with her front teeth before trying to swallow them whole. I could tell from looking at her that the dry cakes were stuck in her throat. I offered her the bottle of water, and she hid the plastic bag behind her back before taking a long swig. Then she seemed to come to her senses. She let out a long breath and sat down for a moment before handing the bag and bottle back to me. 'You should eat too,' she said.

'Please have the rest, Grandmother.'

She slowly ate them, one at a time. When the bag was empty, she offered it to me again. I stood to leave. Chilsung read my intent and started heading toward the tracks. 'Run off now,' she said. 'There's no one left here anymore.'

On the way to Puryong, I ran into countless ghosts wandering the fields and villages every night. Each time they brushed past me on those empty village roads, I heard a low, spooky *woooooo*, like a heavy wind blowing through giant trees. Later, when I travelled to other parts of the world and saw numerous cities and glittering lights and the vitality of those crowds of people, I was struck with disappointment and disgust at how they had all abandoned us and looked the other way.

~

Ah, now we come to that awful day. The day of the inferno.

Chilsung and I were lost somewhere between Chayu Peak and Mount Goseong, outside of Puryong, when we smelled smoke. Chilsung started barking wildly. We were about to head down the mountain, but a strong wind suddenly gusted over us, and smoke rose up all over the ridge. When we went around a bend in the path, we saw that the lower half of the mountain was on fire. No, not just the mountain: all of Heaven and Earth was aflame. The air filled with the smoke of live trees burning, and the crackling of branches and popping of sparks sounded close at hand. The fire was still down at the bottom, but the flames were climbing fast.

I turned and headed uphill. Walking downhill hadn't

been too difficult, but the path back up left me breathless and my legs weak. I glanced back to see the blaze leaping up and being swept forward on the wind. The flames seemed to lap at a hillock on the other side of a narrow ravine. The smoke surrounded us and made it impossible to find our way. I climbed as fast as I could, but the fire was faster. Chilsung kept pausing to look back at me, his tongue lolling out of his mouth. By the time we made it to the top of the ridge, the flames had already reached the spot where we'd stopped to change direction.

I looked down at where we had been headed. The fire seemed to have started at the foot of the mountain: the flames skirted the hem and appeared to be climbing their way up through the folds. White smoke rose from the lower slopes that jutted out between the narrow ravines and long stretches of open field. Something was moving fast through the underbrush: several roe deer and water deer were on the run. They stopped at the top for a moment and glanced at us before springing over the ridge. A line of flame reached the western ridge and began to climb upward. Luckily, as there weren't many trees, it had only weeds and small shrubs to feed on. But once it was joined by the rest of the flames coming up from below, the fire would spread to the summit in an instant.

I followed the deer over the ridge with Chilsung and sat down on the grass and dried leaves so I could slide down the steep slope of the mountain like a playground slide. The slope ended abruptly, and my body was aloft. I slammed into a tree branch, ricocheted off it, and hit the ground. My body was soaked with sweat, and the pain in my side from where

I had collided with the branch made it hard to breathe. It turned out that smoke was coming up from below on that side as well. Chilsung pressed his ears back and began to growl and snarl. A family of wild boar came bounding down the slope after us. They balked when they saw us, turned tail and vanished downhill, the babies scrambling to keep up with their parents. Chilsung growled and took off after them.

Stupid dog! They won't hurt us! They're trying to escape too!

I stood up to try to follow them, but couldn't draw a breath. I must have pulled a muscle in my side, or possibly broken a rib. The pain went away after a few days, but even after I made it back across the Tumen River, it was another month before I stopped getting a stitch in my side every time I walked. I planted my hands on the ground and crawled on all fours through the underbrush, like the boars. The ground turned rocky, and I came upon a ravine where a stream of water was burbling down through the rocks.

Acrid smoke carried on the wind began to fill the ravine. The flames were now at the upper reaches of the slope. The crackling of dry branches catching fire sounded very close. I crouched down behind a large boulder where the water had pooled. The small puddle held no more than about two large bowls' worth of water.

The flames zigzagged down the slope, following the trees and the curve of the mountain, while the ravine acted like a chimney, channelling the wind and narrowing the approaching column of smoke and fire. Already I could feel the heat pressing down, and it became harder and harder to breathe. Though I'd never been taught what to do in a fire, I dunked my clothes in the water, wrapped my wet jacket around my head and lay as flat as I could behind the boulder. The trees directly overhead shivered and shook and caught flame. Despite the wet clothes covering me, my back burned like I was standing too close to a campfire. The smoke, the smells, the spattering of pine resin and tree bark as they burned and the whoosh of the flames buoyed by the strong wind soared up through the ravine. I squeezed my eyes shut, but my face still wound up covered in tears and snot, and I could not stop coughing. When I finally raised my head the fire had passed, and only small embers were floating around; smoke rose from what was left of the trees. It was starting to get dark. We were on the north side of the mountain, so the sun would set even faster. The ground was spotted red with glowing embers, and burned-out stumps illuminated the ashes around them like blocks of charcoal inside a furnace. Small columns of smoke rose from the ground, and as it grew darker I felt as if I was standing in the middle of Hell. I could still hear some trees burning. A tall larch on fire stood on the slope like a giant torch, its flaming branches spreading out in all directions.

'Chilsung-*ah*! Chilsung-*ah*!' I called out as I limped down the ravine.

My voice echoed all around. Just as I had done once before, I focused my mind on trying to picture his location. He wasn't far. I wandered among the rocks, looking for him. I finally spotted his body collapsed on a patch of grass, not far from the water's edge. When Chilsung saw me, he wagged his tail weakly. *Are you hurt?* I said. *Can you get up?* But it seemed he no longer had the strength to communicate his thoughts to me. His white fur was streaked with ash, and I saw then that blood was pouring out of an angry red gash in his belly. The blood had turned the underside of his fur red, and was soaking the ground. Who would be stupid enough to go after some wild boars who were only trying to get their babies to safety?! Maybe he'd thought he was protecting me from them. Of course the mother and father boar would have defended themselves to the death against this intruder. The boar's sharp tusks had ripped open Chilsung's belly. Then, to make matters worse, the fire had passed right over him. I cradled Chilsung's head in my arms and stifled the sound of my crying.

You're all the family I had left in this world, and now I have to go it alone.

For the next few days, as I made my way back to Musan, the mountains continued to burn and send up smoke. I didn't find out how the wildfires had started until after I'd crossed the border again and was in Yanji. They said there were many forest fires all over the world that year. In North Korea, the land was so parched that some of the fires happened on their own, but others were started deliberately. As the famine swept through the country and more and more people starved to death, no one could be stopped from setting fires in the mountains. All the crops had already been harvested from the collective farms and rations had been cut off, so people resorted to creating small slash-and-burn plots for themselves in the mountains. They would slip a pack of matches into their pocket, find a slope or a ravine where no one could see them, and drop a lit match before making a quick getaway.

Even with wildfires blazing so close by, none of the villages had the manpower left to do anything about it. Once a fire began, it would burn for several days, sometimes as long as a week, until all the mountains nearby had burned too. When the dense forests were reduced to ash, people scrambled to stake out their plots and dig up the burned tree stumps to create open fields. There they planted corn and potatoes. Those who cultivated these slash-and-burn fields survived the following year.

I made my way back across the Tumen River, back to where I'd started my journey, pausing at every peak to look behind me at the smoke rising from mountains both near and far. It looked like distress signals sent to distant passing ships from people trapped on desert islands in the middle of a boundless ocean. The smoke rose to the sky in silent, ominously thick clouds, and the sound I'd heard, the whoosh of air rushing past on a night thronged with ghosts, seemed to lay heavy across the land.

FIVE

After I failed to make it all the way to Puryong in search of my parents, and then lost Chilsung on top of that, I returned to the dugout hut in silence. When I stepped inside, I discovered that a disgusting old badger had taken up residence. I searched for a long stick that I could use to try to drive it out, but he was a ferocious little guy: he kept blocking my stick with his paws and lunging at me in fury. His shrill cry was terrifying, but I was no less tough, having already faced certain death and prevailed more than once. I chased out the badger, cleaned up the little hut, dug up the cache of grain that I'd buried in the woods, and proceeded to hunker down for the next month or so, until one day I heard someone moving around outside. It was the farmer. He pulled back the piece of vinyl covering the door and poked his head in.

'*Ya!* Look who's here! You're still alive!'

His eyes reddened with tears, and he clasped my hand tight. I went with him back to the farmhouse. The family already knew about Hyun's death and Father's departure. I told them all about Grandmother dying, my going back to

North Korea to search for the rest of my family, and losing Chilsung. The farmer's wife and his mother turned their backs and wept.

'See,' the farmer's mother said, 'you have to carry on for your family's sake. Someone has to survive to tell the story.'

I stayed with them for nearly a month. My cheeks plumped back up, and my hair regained its lustre. The farmer contacted Uncle Salamander, who said he would find work for me, and then he personally escorted me all the way past Helong to downtown Yanji. There, we waited in a teahouse for Uncle Salamander. His potbelly had grown bigger since the last time I'd seen him, and he was wearing a baggy windbreaker. He told us that after the famine started the authorities had cracked down on cross-border trade, so he'd started a small travel agency for South Korean tourists with someone instead. The three of us went out to eat. Uncle Salamander and the farmer bought me food while they filled each other in on everything that had happened. Uncle Salamander downed several shots of *soju* before turning to me.

'I'm sorry I wasn't there for you. That's how it goes, I guess. I kept telling myself I would check in on you guys, but easier said than done. In any case, think of me as your family now. Don't hesitate to come to me anytime you need my help.'

I finished eating and decided to risk a question while the men were still drinking.

'My sister Mi crossed over before the rest of us. If she's still here, I'd like to try to find her.'

'Ah yes, I remember. I know some people who might

have leads. I'll see what I can find out.'

Uncle Salamander found me a job working for a Han Chinese family. The parents were both teachers. I spent six months as a live-in housekeeper and babysitter before moving on to Paradise, the massage studio where I would later work. While living with the family, I learned a little Chinese. The woman gave me a primary-school textbook and helped me learn how to read and write. When I moved out, she patted me on the back.

'You're a clever one, Bari,' she said. 'You'll do well wherever you go. I've never seen a student learn as quickly as you do.'

The job at Paradise was also thanks to Uncle Salamander — except I wasn't supposed to call him that anymore. I said it to his face without thinking, and he rapped me on the head with his knuckles and gently scolded me: 'Little cheeky to call your uncle by a nickname, no? Your father's the only person left who gets to call me that.' It made me sad to hear that.

He told me that if I wanted to make a lot of money without too much risk, then I should learn a trade at a business run by one of his younger friends. I was well aware that most North Koreans in my position weren't paid for their work — they were grateful if they got so much as room and board. The police were not yet actively hunting down defectors, but they did show up if complaints were made. Regardless of the type of work they did, North Koreans earned no more than a third of what a documented Chinese resident might earn; but I was lucky, and earned half, and that was for doing mostly small errands as an apprentice.

Paradise, which specialised in foot massage, was surrounded by bars and karaoke parlours. There were massage studios nearby that doubled as saunas and gave full-body massages, but they charged more than us and were rumoured to offer more than just a rubdown. Our place was frequented mostly by tourists and business travellers. Married couples also came by sometimes to get foot massages together. Paradise was where I met Xiang. There were around twenty masseuses in total, with Korean Chinese working alongside Han Chinese. Most were young, unmarried women who'd come from distant rural villages to earn money in the city. Of the six who were married, only two actually lived with their husbands. The married women were no different from the rest in that they'd left their hometowns and come to Yanji in search of work, either alone or with only their children in tow. Xiang was one of the two who lived with her husband. She must have been around twenty-five years old at the time. The oldest was Qinqin, who had her kids with her and claimed she was thirty, but according to Ms Kim, the old Korean-Chinese auntie who took care of the cooking and cleaning, she was closer to thirty-four. The owner of the studio would show up around closing time to dole out everyone's daily wages, while his wife ran the business the rest of the time.

Our biggest rush was always right after lunch or late at night. During the slack hours of the late afternoons and early evenings, the masseuses would gather in the lobby and pass the time snacking and watching television. Sometimes Ms Kim and I would throw together a simple dish for them. We minded the owners, but the ones we really had to be good to were the masseuses, because they would sometimes split their tips with us.

———

One day, while cleaning the showers, I found a gold ring. I'd just sprayed detergent on the tiled walls, given them a good scrub and was rinsing the suds off with the handheld showerhead when I noticed something shiny in the drain trap. I bent over to take a closer look. The sizeable gold ring had a square face with a lotus flower engraved in the middle. I slipped it on. The ring spun loosely around my finger. I wondered who'd lost it. Given the size, it would be worth a lot if I sold it in the night market. I stashed it in my apron pocket. The following morning, after everyone had arrived for work and I was carrying trays of food back and forth to serve them their lunch, I paused for a moment and asked for everyone's attention.

'Excuse me, did one of you lose something?' I asked.

The Korean-Chinese women translated what I'd said for the Han Chinese women sitting next to them. They looked at each other in silence, and then Xiang raised her hand.

'Did you find my ring?' she asked me in Chinese.

I answered in Chinese: 'What does it look like?'

'Well, it's gold ... and it has a lotus flower engraved on the front.'

I smiled and pulled the ring from my pocket. A few days later, Xiang slipped a bill, folded neatly into a square, into my hand after one of her massage appointments. I went to the kitchen and unfolded it. It was a twenty-*yuan* note. I'd received one-*yuan* and five-*yuan* tips before, but never so much at one time. When Xiang finished with a difficult massage and was resting in the lobby, I brought her some warm, sweet jujube tea. That's how we became friends.

One Sunday, when she had a day off, Xiang got permission from the owner to take me to her house. She lived in a small flat with a front room and a kitchenette near the Eastern Market. Even before we reached her door, I could smell food cooking. As soon as we stepped inside, I saw a man standing at the kitchen counter with his back to us. He was dressed in a sleeveless undershirt and was stir-frying meat and vegetables in a wok.

'I'm home!' Xiang called out.

Xiang's husband kept flipping the food in the wok and said, without turning to look at us: 'Welcome back. Did you bring Bari with you?'

We sat down in the front room, which was furnished with only a table and four chairs. When he brought out the food he'd prepared, I stood and introduced myself timidly. I tried to help him with the food, but Xiang tugged me back by the hem of my shirt. She seemed to be saying that, in their house, whoever started a task had to finish it. They were Han Chinese, so of course the food was Chinese too. There were two types of stir-fried vegetables, pork, and fried fish. They were chatty and talked fast, but I was only able to manage a few simple words.

Xiang's husband, Zhou, listened as she told him my story, and then he told me how they'd left their hometown in Heilongjiang Province together. He had worked there as an assistant to a doctor of traditional Chinese medicine while learning acupuncture from him, and recently he'd been taking classes at a private institute to get certified as an acupuncturist. Then he would be able to move to a larger city and make more money. Each time he smiled, his sparse facial hair made his mouth look huge, and his eyes, which were much smaller in contrast, looked like two lines drawn in pencil.

'He taught me the meridian points for the feet,' Xiang said.

'Meridian points?'

'They're not visible to the naked eye, but every part of the human body is connected to a point on the bottom of your feet.'

Xiang poked her husband and told him to stick his foot out. He reluctantly offered up his dirty foot, and Xiang pointed to different spots with a ballpoint pen, identifying meridian points for the heart, stomach, and liver. It was hard for me to understand all of it.

'You should learn this, Bari. You could make good money giving massages.'

'I would like to.'

Xiang and her husband talked amongst themselves for a moment.

'Let's see if we can get permission from the owner for you to come home with me on Sundays,' Xiang said. 'There's so much to learn about feet. In the meantime, I'll teach you foot massage techniques whenever there's downtime at work.'

I'd never told anyone outside of my family about my strange gift. I'd never even told Uncle Salamander, who was practically my legal guardian, about having talked to ghosts while searching for my parents in Puryong. I wanted people to see me as a normal, ordinary girl. Of course, I also never told anyone that I was from North Korea, and even at work, if anyone so much as alluded to it, the boss scolded them: 'Bad enough if she gets caught and taken away, but we'll also get shut down and fined. Which means you'll all be out of work too!'

Every Sunday, I went to Xiang's flat and learned meridian points on the foot from Zhou. Xiang would sit down and prop her feet up, and Zhou would point out different spots on the bottom of her feet and explain them to me. He had three different short, wooden sticks that he used to massage feet: one had a rounded tip, another looked like a small chisel and the third was pointier. But most of what I learned was with my bare hands. He taught me how to use the flat of my thumb as well as the tip; how to use the whole length of my fingers; how to make a fist and lightly punch or press my knuckles into the sole of the foot; to press and slap with the palm of my hand; to use both hands to knead the foot; and to pinch, rotate, and loosen the muscles in the ankle and the joints of the toes. Zhou told me that while the wooden tools made the job easier, using your bare hands to give a foot massage was much more effective.

'See, just as the rest of the body consists of different parts, the foot is divided into three sections: the sole, the instep, and the heel and ankle. It's the same with the hands, so it's more effective if you start with a light hand massage before working on their feet. The meridian points for the internal organs are clustered in the sole and the heel, and the points for the head are in the toes. The arch of the foot, here, is the kidneys. The padded part just below the fourth and fifth toes of the left foot corresponds to the heart. On the right foot, it's the liver.'

Zhou demonstrated all of this on Xiang's feet and explained it to me again using my own feet. Then he had me practise on him. Whenever I made a mistake, he lifted up his foot to explain again before having me continue. I did this every Sunday as I studied the meridian points on the feet. I memorised the ten steps for relaxing the hands, and the fifteen basic moves for massaging the feet, before moving on to the main meridian points for healing illnesses. Zhou taught me everything by example. 'A customer comes in drunk,' he would say. 'What do you do?'

'The meridian points for the head are concentrated in the big toe, so I would start by applying acupressure to each toe in turn to relieve his headache. Then I would rub the sole of the foot, which corresponds to the intestines, and the heel, to help stimulate the liver and kidneys …'

After eight months at Paradise, I became a masseuse. As I was not a documented resident with a Chinese family registration, I wasn't officially licensed to practise massage; it was my skill alone that qualified me to take customers. I also wasn't given a commission the way the other masseuses were, and was paid only in whatever tips I received; but the tips were much better than what I'd made before from running errands and helping out with cooking.

After becoming a masseuse, I realised that I was able to tell what was wrong with a person just by studying their face and touching their feet. It began with my very first customer, a Chinese man. He was husky and a little overweight. After stripping down to his undershirt and rolling up the legs of his suit trousers, he sprawled out on the massage table with his legs dangling over the side. I washed his feet with a mixture of lukewarm water and salt and vinegar, and then let them soak in a bowl of hot water steeped with mugwort while I slowly massaged his calves. I dried his feet off with a towel and started with his left foot. I began by applying pressure to the meridian points on each toe in turn, just as I'd been taught, but his heel had a strange red glow coming from it: I knew at once that something was wrong with his liver and intestines.

Next was an older female tourist. This time, not only were the soles of her feet glowing red and blue, but as I rubbed and thumped her feet I closed my eyes and started to see something: a car, crossing a bridge. Suddenly a truck came racing up from behind, slamming into it. The small car lay upside down in the road, the frame half crumpled. I stopped and leaned over to whisper in the ear of the Korean-Chinese woman working beside me.

'I think this woman was in a car accident.'

'Why? Does she have a weird scar or something?'

'No, it's not that …'

Some of my customers picked up on the fact that I was good at finding the parts of their feet that needed extra attention, and they became my regulars. Xiang, as well, had guessed there was something different about me, but she assumed it was just that I had an unnatural aptitude for the job.

—

Two years after I first came to Paradise, I turned fifteen and moved to Dalian with Xiang and her husband. Zhou had earned his acupuncture licence and was going into business with a friend who'd opened a foot massage studio there. I felt it was my duty to break the news to Uncle Salamander properly, so I called him up and invited him out to dinner.

'Oh my,' he laughed. 'Our little Bari is all grown up now.'

It wasn't easy scheduling dinner with him. Since he worked as both a travel agent and a tour guide, he was busy ferrying visitors from the airport to their hotels every day and personally driving the small sightseeing bus that shuttled tourists to Mount Baekdu.

He asked me to meet him at a restaurant specialising in skewered lamb. Branches had opened up all over the country. Lamb meat was threaded onto long, metal skewers and rotated over a hot grill using an apparatus that had been invented by an army veteran. Uncle Salamander got there before me. When I arrived, he waved me over to where he was sitting in a booth. He kept dabbing at his sweaty face with a wet wipe.

'Everything okay?' he asked. 'Still getting a lot of customers?'

'Yes, as a matter of fact, we've been short of hands lately and had to hire more masseuses.'

'Good, good. I think I need a drink.'

I pulled the cooked lamb from the skewer and set it on

his plate as he poured himself a shot of *soju*.

'How old are you now?'

'Fifteen.'

'Fifteen already! How time does fly!'

'Uncle, I need to tell you something.'

I told him about Xiang and her husband, and how they were like family to me now, just like him, and that they were planning to move to Dalian and open a massage studio and so I'd decided to go with them. He nodded.

'Since you say they're good people, I suppose I can trust them. Do you owe Paradise any money?'

I shook my head.

'But have you told your boss?'

'Not yet. I wanted to discuss it with you first.'

Uncle Salamander waved his hands at me and brought his finger up to his lips.

'Don't breathe a word of it. Just slip out of there when the time comes. Someone in your situation can't afford to trust anyone. Keep your guard up from now on. Even in this town, people aren't as friendly as they used to be. Do you know why? Money. No matter where you go in the world, it's always the same. The electric lights go on, money comes in, and kindness vanishes. All the young guys from the North that I used to trade with have become pimps.'

Uncle Salamander took another shot of *soju* and leaned his head back.

'They make a living by selling girls like you. Which reminds me: I found your sister.'

'Mi? Where is she?'

He told me he'd tracked her down a long time earlier,

101

through a younger colleague who owned a bar in Longjing.

'I told him I was looking for a girl from Musan and mentioned your father's name and position. That's how I found out where she is.'

I set my chopsticks down and was already halfway out of my seat.

'Let's go to her now!'

'Hold on, there's more to the story. Do you really think I would've stopped there?'

It seems the moment Mi crossed the Tumen River, she was scooped up by human traffickers and sold to a Han Chinese man in a village about sixty *li* outside of Longjing. Uncle Salamander was too bogged down with work to go look for her right away, but when some business came up that took him to Kaishantun, he set out to find her with only the name of the village written on a scrap of paper.

The place that greeted him at the end of the winding dirt road, dust clouds billowing around him as he went, was a remote mountain village. There were a dozen homes there, with both Han Chinese and Korean Chinese. When he asked around about my sister Mi, a Korean-Chinese woman cautiously pointed to one of the houses. The two-room house, which was on the verge of collapsing, had a chicken coop to the side of the courtyard, a pen where they were raising pigs, and corn and bean fields that started right behind the house and stretched back quite a way. At least it looked like they never had to go hungry.

'I'm pretty sure the only things of value in that shack were the piglets. They probably sold one to buy Mi. There was an old man loafing around in the courtyard, and I could hear a child bawling inside the house.'

Uncle Salamander said he'd combed his hair very neatly and wore a green jacket so he would look like a government official. He cleared his throat loudly and told the old man that he'd heard a North Korean girl was living there. When he asked where she was, the old man got angry and retorted that they'd spent good money on her only to have her run away. He said his son had gone searching for her all over, but the bastards who sold her to them said she wasn't in China anymore.

'I didn't want to tell you this part, but your sister had a baby with that man. The situation must have been really bad for her to abandon her child like that. As far as I can tell, she's nowhere to be found anywhere near Yanji. In fact, you never know — she might have fled to South Korea. That would be a small mercy.'

I'd come to the restaurant expecting nothing, but there I was, crying my eyes out in front of strangers for the first time in my life. I realised at last how numb I had become to the loss of my family. Or maybe I was crying over my own fate.

I took my uncle's advice and did not say a word to my boss about leaving. Every day that week, when Xiang clocked out, I packed a few of my belongings and sent them with her, and that Sunday I got permission to go home with her again. The next day, the three of us boarded a train.

Dalian filled us with hope. The waterfront was beautiful, the city was clean and the parks were really well designed. Zhou's friend, Chen, was originally from Dalian and had experience managing a sauna in Yanji. He'd purchased a commercial building on a small side street off of Anshan Street, one of the main roads downtown, and had redone the interior. It was an old, three-storey building, but the ivy climbing up the grey walls made it look nice. There was a restaurant on the first floor, and the foot massage studio was on the second floor. We rented a two-room flat on the third floor.

There were so many people looking for work in the city that when we posted job adverts in the newspaper and a local weekly magazine, women gathered like clouds. Xiang, Zhou, and Chen sat inside, behind a desk, while I waited on a chair outside the door and called out names from the résumés we'd collected. The women were queued up all the way down the stairs, waiting to be interviewed. The top five all had massage experience, and we hired twenty more because they were pretty and looked like they were in good health. Chen told me only ten of them would end up employed. He was right: during the first week of training, led by Xiang and Zhou, five slipped out the exit and never came back. Then, when it was time for the grand opening, Xiang sent away five more who hadn't shown any improvement.

Chen and Zhou printed up flyers and distributed them in bars, restaurants, and teahouses. They charged much less than the fancy hotels, which had large saunas that offered both full-body and foot massages. Chen, drawing on his management experience, hired some teenagers who were loafing around nearby and offered them a commission on any customers they brought in. Zhou set up a separate room off to the side, where he provided acupuncture and cupping. We didn't get the rich customers that the hotels got, but we did get small shop owners and people in town on business. Chen also went around to motels and inns and drew in visitors who were there on group tours. We made pretty good money for being a brand-new business. Chen had already become something of a community leader in the neighbourhood.

———

When I look back now on how I wound up crossing the ocean and coming all the way to England, I can't help but blame my name. Grandmother told me the story of Princess Bari every night in our cosy little dugout hut, but it wasn't until after I was on that ship that I thought about the princess going west in search of the life-giving water — out where the sun sets.

One day, Xiang and I were up on the third floor, sleeping in late, when we heard men arguing loudly downstairs. Their voices were punctuated by the sound of glass breaking. Startled, our eyes opened wide, and we heard a man's high-pitched scream. It was Zhou. Xiang and I looked at each other, sprang out of bed and ran downstairs in our bare feet. The door to the massage studio was wide open. The first things I saw were glass shards and goldfish writhing and flapping around on the cement floor: the fishbowl had been knocked off the table. Four men stood over Zhou, who was sprawled on the floor, blood pouring from his head. Xiang shielded him with her body and yelled at the men.

'Who are you? How dare you hit him?'

One of them, a short, chubby man in his fifties, shook a

piece of paper at her.

'Do you know what this is? It's a promissory note. You think you can borrow someone else's money and not pay it back?'

Xiang shook her husband and gave him a searching look. He grimaced and answered weakly: 'I didn't know either. They say Chen borrowed money from them.'

'Why are you responsible for Chen's debts?'

In response to Xiang's sharp tone, the older man let out a guffaw.

'Because he borrowed it under this shop's name. You are business partners, aren't you?'

A man with a shaved head pointed the jagged neck of a broken bottle at us and said: 'Not even the deposit on this pathetic business of yours will be enough to pay back the principal.' Then he flung the broken bottle away.

Zhou, who'd already been on the receiving end of the bottle, cowered and crawled into Xiang's arms. The men — back-alley loan sharks — threw open the doors and rummaged through every cabinet, going all the way up to the third floor, as if tallying up the value of every item and piece of furniture in the building.

The older man took off his suit jacket and unbuttoned his shirt.

'Come sit here,' he said to Zhou. 'The rest of you should get lost.'

He glared at us as he said this, but instead Xiang dragged her husband over to the spot he'd indicated and crouched firmly beside him.

'Both of our lives depend on this shop,' she said, 'so

'whatever you say is meant for my ears, too.'

'Very well. I have two suggestions for you. Pay back the full amount of the loan before the end of the month, or pay off the principal with interest month by month.' Zhou was speechless.

'What's the full amount?' Xiang asked.

'One and a half million.'

I couldn't even fathom that much money. One serving of three dumplings cost one *yuan* — this was my dinner when times were hard. Xiang stared off into space and laughed in shock.

'And if we can't pay you back?' she asked.

'You'll pay us back with your bodies.'

Xiang and I were at a loss for words.

'We need more time,' Zhou said quietly.

'More time? Don't try to worm your way out of this.'

'I own a small plot of land back in my hometown that I can use as collateral for a loan, but I'll need time.'

The man thought this over for a moment; then he rose, buttoned up his shirt, and put his jacket back on.

'Fine. You have exactly three days.'

'My hometown is all the way in Heilongjiang Province. It'll take me three days just to get there and back.'

'Yeah? Then I'll give you two extra days. But if I come back in five days and you still don't have my money, I'll gouge your eyes out.'

After the men left, we all sat slumped on the floor and cried quietly. I was crying from fear, but Xiang and Zhou were probably weeping at having their dreams shattered. Then we heard footsteps coming up the stairs, and the bald man who'd threatened us with the broken bottle came back in. He handed two train tickets to Zhou.

'Economy. Looks like I'll be suffering too, because of you.'

Even after Zhou and the bald man had left for the station, Xiang and I didn't bother to clean up. We went up to the third floor and sat there in a trance. In the afternoon the masseuses started reporting for work, and came to find us with confused looks on their faces. Xiang barely summoned the strength to send them home, saying we would be closed for a few days.

Early the following morning, we heard someone banging on the door downstairs. Zhou had returned with the bald man, who entered right behind him. The two of them had been drinking. The bald man was red-faced, but otherwise sober, whereas Zhou was dead drunk. Neither had much to say. Xiang and I guessed that they'd come to some sort of agreement, but we had no idea what. Zhou whispered to us to pack our clothes for a trip. He wouldn't explain why. I threw a few toiletries, underwear, and clothing into a bag and followed them. We slipped out without anyone seeing us and crossed Changjiang Road, where we caught a taxi about a block away from our building. We headed to the north side of Dalian Bay to the train station near Ganjingzi Park. The bald man walked ahead and led us to a cheap motel down a dark, muddy alley. The room was cramped and dark, and even the wallpaper was black with dirt. It was the kind of place that was mostly used by migrant workers from other provinces. The bald man disappeared again without a word.

'What on earth are you up to?' Xiang demanded.

'We can't stay here anymore,' Zhou said. 'We have to leave China.'

Zhou had gone to Dalian Station with the bald man in tow to keep a close eye on him. While waiting for the train, he had pleaded for their lives. The bald man listened silently and then asked how much the deposit was on their building, and whether or not Zhou could get it. His change of heart was not out of pity. He was just tired of performing menial tasks in exchange for a few coins from his boss, and was thinking about going into business for himself.

The man asked Zhou if he knew what 'snakeheads' were. Back in Yanji, Chen had told Zhou over drinks one night about these gangs of smugglers who worked at the harbour. Zhou remembered that people smuggled out of the country were referred to as 'snakes'. The bald man told him the down payment was at least five thousand dollars per snake. Anyone who didn't have enough could have their family back home write a promissory note for the balance, and any money made abroad could be sent back to the family to pay down the total debt. The interest was nearly thirty percent. Rumour had it that if you missed a payment, one of your family members' fingers would be cut off and sent to you as warning. After hearing the whole story, Xiang looked shocked.

'Where are we supposed to get that kind of money?' she asked.

'If we can get back our deposit on the store and add it to the cash we've saved, we'll have enough to cover the down payment.'

The following day, Xiang and I stayed locked up in the motel room while Zhou, flanked by the bald man and another man, spent the day downtown.

On our last night in Dalian, the bald man's accomplice showed us where to go. We followed him across the railroad tracks to the wharf. I could hear waves breaking against the sea wall, and even the air was salty. In the dark, the lights of a fishing boat switched on and then the engine roared to life. Faint, shadowy figures appeared. As I stepped closer to the boat, two hands reached down over the side.

'Grab hold,' a voice said.

I was pulled up first. My body spilled over the side and into the boat. Xiang followed right behind me, but when Zhou tried to climb up, the man in the boat shoved him away.

'You only paid for two snakes.'

I heard Zhou shouting: 'Xiang! Xiaaang!' into the wind. The man who had taken us to the wharf was holding him back. The engine revved as the boat pulled away. Xiang clung to the side of the boat, howling in misery. The man struck her hard across the face, and Xiang flopped onto the wet deck like a frog.

As she struggled to get up, one of the men said: 'If you make any noise, we'll throw you overboard. Sit there and be quiet.'

The small fishing boat lurched across the harbour to where the large ships were anchored. They pulled up alongside a huge container ship, the sides of which rose up like an enormous wall blocking everything from sight. One of the men pointed a torch up at the deck looming faintly above us and flicked it on and off several times. A dark figure appeared. They called back and forth to each other, and then a rope was lowered. The man who'd been standing at the side of the fishing boat grabbed the rope and tied it around my waist without any explanation. He gave the rope a few tugs, and they started to pull. I dangled in midair, unable even to scream, as they hauled me up. The wind spun me in circles, and my body slammed into the side of the iron ship with a loud clang. As soon as I reached the railing, two men grabbed my arms and pulled me over. I was so dizzy I thought I was going to vomit. They lowered the rope again, and after a moment Xiang was brought up too, her body limp and dangling. Neither of the men said a word to us. They led us into the ship, prodding and shoving us along. Xiang practically had to be dragged. We went down a stairwell with a metal railing and through a low-ceilinged corridor with many high doorsills. I kept stumbling. My knee slammed into a chunk of metal, and blood trickled down my shin. Later, I realised we were in the very bottom of the ship. Freight containers were stacked in neat rows, and there were narrow spaces in between where we could sit with our legs stretched out. In the darkness, I could just make out other people sitting with their backs against the walls. Xiang fell across my lap and sobbed, her shoulders trembling.

'Xiang, are you okay? Are you injured?' I asked.

'Shh!' Someone whispered in the dark. 'Not a word!'

I quieted instantly. The sound of machinery and metal clanging against metal was constant. After what felt like a long wait, the floor seemed to shimmy, and then the boat began to move. We were off. Xiang and I sat against the wall with our heads touching and dozed off. The tremendous fatigue that had been building up over the past several days washed over me at once.

—

Bari-ya! Hey, Bari! It's me!

Someone calls to me through the dark. I see two blue, glowing lights. I know at once that it is Chilsung. I have seen him in my dreams now and then over the past few years, but this is the first time he has spoken to me just as he did in life. A ring of milky-white light, like moonlight, appears in the blackness and wobbles as it widens. At the end of this tunnel of light, Chilsung wags his snowy white tail and waits for me.

He takes off running, glancing back occasionally and pausing so I can catch up.

Stop running, I say. *Stand still.*

Someone's waiting for you.

We reach a riverbank. The water looks black. A silent breeze passes over us and kicks up a cloud of dust. There is a long bridge, and at the entrance to the bridge stands a woman dressed all in white. It is too dark at first to make out her features, but as I step closer a light seems to shine forth from her and a familiar face appears.

Our little Bari is here!

Grandma! Where've you been?

I take a step forward to hug her, but she drifts back exactly one step, lightly, like a plastic bag filled with air. I take another step, and she drifts back again.

I've missed you so much, and now you won't even hug me.

Grandmother smiles and nods.

I know. I wish I could. But I'm in this world now, and you're in that world. I called you here because I was worried about you. Now, pay attention to what I'm about to tell you. You're going to travel thousands and thousands of li *across the ocean and across the sky. This path will lead you through Hell, filled with the clamour of toads and the ravings of demons and the spirits of the dead. You could wind up torn to pieces. But whatever you do, stay away from the blue and yellow paths. Always take the white path. When your journey is complete, you'll no longer be little Bari. You'll be Bari, the great shaman. I will help you as much as I can, so whenever you're in trouble, Chilsung will guide you to me.*

—

Grandmother, Chilsung, and the foggy riverbank vanished, and everything went white before my eyes. Someone was shining a torch at us.

'Raise your hand as you call out your number. Start at that end.'

The man sitting at the far end of the wall raised his hand and said *one*. The woman next to him was slow to react. After a beat, she mumbled *t-two*, and someone stepped in front of the man with the torch and slammed her head against the wall.

'Again!'

This time, everyone called out *three, four, five,* and so on, in quick succession. There were twelve people altogether.

'You little snakes all know your numbers? Those are your names from now on.'

I was Number Eleven, and Xiang was Number Twelve. Judging by the voices, there were four women and eight men.

'I'm the one responsible for getting you safely to your destination. Your lives are in our hands. Don't forget that. If you don't do as we say immediately, we'll throw you overboard. In a few days, we're going to dock briefly at Xiamen, in Fujian Province. Until then, you will not move from this spot. You'll get one meal every morning and one bucket of water that you'll all have to ration. You're each responsible for your own survival. It takes one month to reach England. If you can survive the last ten days, upon arrival, then you'll get to set foot in a new land and make all the money you want. Right before we reach Xiamen, I'll explain what you have to do.'

They gave each of us a single ball of rice and fed us a cup of water. They also designated a spot for us to relieve ourselves: just inside the entrance to the cargo hold in the belly of the ship, they'd set up a metal drum that had been sawed in half and placed a couple of wooden boards over it. At first we all slept sitting up against the walls, but after a while negotiations were made, and everyone was able to sleep lying down in the narrow spaces between the containers by placing their legs between one another's legs. For the first few days it was too dark to see anyone, but later we got just enough light seeping in from above during the day that we were able to learn each other's faces. Twenty more joined us in Xiamen. Like us, they were brought aboard just before the ship departed. We had to stay hidden for two days while more containers were loaded. The snakeheads divided us up and stuffed us inside the already-packed containers. We really were like snakes, as we had to burrow deep into the tiny crevices between the packed freight loads. We had to remain standing the whole time, though we were able to take the weight off of our legs a little bit by wedging our upper bodies in, and we had to urinate and defecate in place as well. There was no food, of course, but we also weren't given so much as a drop of water to drink.

Right before the boat set sail again, we were pulled out of the containers while new people were smuggled aboard. No one could walk. We crawled back to our spots and sprawled out on the floor. When the woman who'd had her head smacked against the wall for not calling her number out properly was brought out of the container, she could not stand up again; somewhere in the South China Sea, she died. The snakeheads picked her up by her head and legs and carried her out. Number Eight grew so weak that she had to be helped to the toilet each time. Xiang and I were still young, and fortunately had a little strength to spare. The people who boarded in Xiamen sat between the rows of containers next to ours; most of them were young, too. There seemed to be about seven or eight women among them. As the ship crossed the equator, we entered the fiery level of Hell, and thirst and starvation slowly turned people into animals.

SIX

I stripped off my shell of a body more than once during those long days of darkness and followed Chilsung down the white path to see my grandmother. Once, after coming to briefly and taking a look around, I realised that the world of the dead was no different from the place I was in. I travelled in the ship through the different layers of the otherworld.

I lay with my eyes closed and my back pressed to the bottom of the ship as it rose and fell with the waves, the din of machinery constant, and let my spirit rise into the air. It was indeed like slipping out of a shell, or removing a garment. It didn't make a sound, but there was a sensation like soft fabric tearing each time I shed my body and drifted about in the dark.

Then Chilsung would appear, his white fur dazzling my eyes as he wagged his tail in front of me. We would walk single-file along the white path that hovered in the blackness like a belt of moonlight. After a long walk, we would arrive at a riverbank, where a light breeze blew and a bridge arched over the river. The water looked black as tar. Only the bridge was illuminated, as if by lamplight, and Grandmother would come across it, the hem of her white skirt swaying.

Bari, come this way.

When Grandmother walked back over the bridge, it lit up with all the colours of the rainbow. Chilsung walked ahead of me. I followed him across this rainbow bridge. Just then, I heard voices coming from the dark water below, voices crying out to be saved. A woman's ragged screams. Weeping and wailing. Groans of pain. A baby bawling. Voices moaning under the lash. Dying breaths. Teeth chattering as voices cried out about the cold. Shrill screams following one after the other, wailing about the heat. Hollow giggles from going mad. I could barely bring myself to cross the bridge.

Don't listen, and don't look down. If you stray from the path, you'll lose all your good karma.

Once I was over the bridge, I saw that the sun was shining there, and everything was strangely quiet. A wide field filled with fresh grass stretched away evenly, and a delicate breeze stirred the wildflowers. Grandmother pointed to a zelkova tree at the far end of the field.

When you get closer to that tree, your guide will appear. Hurry off now.

Grandma, aren't you coming with me?

I can't. My world ends here.

What about Chilsung?

He slowly wagged his tail and didn't answer. Grandmother held out her hand.

Take these with you. It'll help.

She dropped three peony blossoms into my palm. I put them in my pocket and floated over to the tree, bobbing gently as if carried there on a current. The tree was enormous;

117

it had to have been as tall as a three or four-storey building. The branches were completely bare, though it wasn't winter. The closer I got to that tree, with its countless branches twisting out of its thick trunk in all directions, the scarier it looked. On one of the lower branches perched a magpie, flicking its tail. When it saw me it rubbed its beak against the tree several times and then addressed me.

Hey, Stupidhead, where you think you're goin'? Oughta give you what for.

What did I do wrong? I asked angrily. Despite everything that had happened to me up until that point, I had submitted to all of it meekly, without a single word of blame or complaint, sorrow or frustration, so I truly felt this was uncalled-for. The bird opened its beak wide and laughed at me. Then it said:

You're still a long way from bringing back the life-giving water. How the living do suffer, do suffer!

I clamped down on my anger.

Show me the way to the western sky, I said.

Follow me, follow me.

The little featherbrain spread his wings and took off from the tip of the branch, circled overhead several times, and flew straight into the side of the enormous tree trunk as if to crush his own skull.

Serves you right, I thought. *Now you're dead of a busted skull.*

But the trunk opened like a yawning mouth, and the bird disappeared into it. I placed one foot inside the shadowy hollow, and the rest of my body was sucked inside. I slid down, down, down. When I reached the bottom, the top of the tree hovered far above my head and I saw a road stretching out in five directions: north, south, east, west, and centre. In the middle of the road stood an envoy from the otherworld, dressed all in black and wearing a black horsehair hat. He clutched a folding fan with both hands. *Where are you going?* he asked.

I'd been wondering the same thing, so I had no response at first. But then I said the first thing that came to mind:

They told me to come over for dinner.

The envoy considered this for a moment and then asked: *The great kings?*

I didn't know what else to do, so I nodded. He pointed to one of the paths with his fan. I walked for a long time and eventually reached a large plaza with torchlight glowing on all sides. The same envoy appeared again and dragged me to the centre. A huge, towering platform, like a judge's bench, appeared along the opposite wall. Seated atop the platform were ten great kings, each with a different type of crown: a horned crown; an ornament-covered crown that stuck straight up like a chimney and gradually widened; a round crown; a wide, flat crown; a crown that bulged out on the sides. The great kings seemed to stir, and then the one seated in the middle wearing the horned crown glared fiercely at me from above his black beard. He called out:

Loathsome worm! You're not dead, yet you dare call us forth in your dreams?

The great king with a white beard and a crown with triangular horns yelled:

You lied and said we invited you here!

The great king with the flat crown said:

We cannot send you back to the flesh you abandoned!

Another said:

An insignificant speck like you arrogantly vows to take the life-giving water from the ends of the Earth?!

The great kings of the otherworld called out my crimes each in turn, and at the very end the king with the round crown said:

You are guilty of abandoning your starving kinsmen. Even if you spend the rest of your life offering food and reciting sutras to the spirits of these dead, you will never wash away your sin!

The ten kings called out their judgement in unison:

Seven by seven is forty-nine. If you can endure forty-nine days of penance, you will be permitted to return.

As soon as their judgement came down, the envoy grabbed me by the nape of the neck, dragged me to the edge of a cliff, and tossed me over. At the bottom of the cliff was a blazing inferno. I screamed long and loud as my body tumbled like a piece of straw down toward the flames, which wriggled like the jaws of a creature intent on swallowing me whole. Just then I remembered the flowers my grandmother had given me. I took one peony from my pocket and tossed it down. With a loud *pop!* the fire vanished, and something like a warm blanket or a cloud wrapped around me. I drifted slowly down through the air.

When I alighted onto the ground, the air filled with a faint blue light and grey smoke billowed all around. A clump of smoke wafted over to me and moaned as it brushed past.

Feed me. Just one bite. Please.

Another clump of smoke coiled around me.

Just one little gaetteok. *Or even some porridge or thin gruel will do.*

The smoke began to fill the large hollow; each clump bore the face it had worn in life. I saw the woman and two children I'd met in the village near Gomusan, as well as the old woman I'd come across at the train station. Countless other faces I'd never seen, and did not know, crowded around me. There were three or four little urchins who'd slept under stairwells in a night market in Yanji, and even babies joined the throng as tiny puffs cleaving to mother clouds. Their eyes were dark, their cheeks sunken, and their throats strangely long and thin. Their mumbling sounded like magic spells: *Hungry, hungry, hungry. Feed me, feed me, feed me.*

I couldn't breathe, my chest was heavy, and my eardrums felt like they were going to burst. I covered my ears with my hands and squatted down on my heels. Then, without thinking about it, I pulled out another peony and tossed it upward. The air filled with wooden bowls packed with steaming hot rice, freshly cooked rice cakes piled high with mashed sweet red beans, every kind of fish and meat, fritters and savoury pancakes, wild greens, stews and soups of every flavour and colour and variety, plates and dishes and platters and saucers galore. All around me I heard the sound of lips smacking and teeth chomping.

Words — half-song, half-incantation — burst out of me, and even in the midst of singing, I recognised them as *Hwangcheon muga*, the shaman song to console the spirits of the dead. It was from the story my grandmother used to tell me about Princess Bari:

121

Aah, aah, deceased spirits!
At this open door between our worlds,
I pray, I pray.
To the mountains, to the rivers
you prayed, you prayed.
Hungry ghosts, starved spirits,
what became of the bodies you wore only yesterday?
Return! Return!
Go to Paradise, come back to life.
You are without sin;
lay down your burdens.

When the song ended, the smoke retreated, low to the ground, and vanished. Suddenly the floor of the hollow tree split in two to reveal a fog-covered pond. A breeze lifted the fog and the glassy, mirror-like surface of the water appeared. The water was the blue-green of moss, and under it a shadow was moving. Against this solid blue screen, images slowly began to take shape:

A stormy sea. A single boat tosses like a leaf amid mountainous waves, barely making it from crest to crest. It is a fishing boat with a squat cabin like a tiny house sticking out of the top. The belly of the ship is stuffed with the day's catch. In that cramped space, where the ceiling is so low that a person can't even sit straight up, water sloshes and rises. Then I notice the people squirming inside. Men, women, children. Ten, twenty, maybe thirty or more. Waves surge over the side of the boat, sweep over the deck and pour down into the hold. Women and children struggle and try to crawl out. The crewmen kick and shove them back in. They close the hatch and padlock it. The wind and waves subside, and the sea is sunny. A distant mountain peak in a foreign land appears on the horizon. The crew remove the dead bodies from the hold and toss them into the sea. Bodies sink below the surface, bob back up, are swept along by the waves.

The coast of a foreign country. A boat, half-sunk and listing. Vegetable crates floating in the water. A large ship approaches. Uniformed people board the boat. They open the crates. Amid the tomatoes and cabbage are drowned bodies.

People suffering and struggling to breathe inside a dark container. The face of a woman clawing at the walls looms large. People crowd the door. They search for any crack in the walls before collapsing in the spaces between the cargo.

People called to the crewmen's tiny quarters. When they are told to hand over more cash, they shake their heads and say they have none. The crewmen begin beating them. They punch their faces, kick their stomachs, gang up on them. Eyes fill with rage. Moneyless men slump to the ground, their faces bloodied. Women's clothes are torn off. The men take turns. The women shake their heads from side to side, cry, struggle.

A narrow alley. Women alight from cars. Heavily made-up faces stare down from every window and every corner. The owner counts heads. Gives money to the men who brought them. Men lick their fingers and count their cash. The women are herded into a curtained room. The owner strips and inspects them.

A woman crouches and covers her mouth to keep from crying, crumpled skirt and top clutched to her naked body. Her face blurs and begins to shake with laughter. She's lost her mind.

She stumbles down a road as if drunk. A young man chases her and smacks her face mercilessly. She's dragged away by the hair and disappears down a filthy alley.

A dark basement. A single fluorescent bulb hangs from a low ceiling. Women sit at sewing machines and stitch together mountains of fabric. Men walk up and down the rows, their hands idle behind their backs.

A storage room at the back of a restaurant piled high with vegetables and shellfish. Water sloshing underfoot. Men trimming cabbage and cleaning fish.

Another stormy sea. Men who have been gathering

clams stand on a tiny sandbank, naked beneath their raingear. They bring their hands to their mouths to shout. The tide rises. The sandbank slowly vanishes and the water rises from stomach to chest. The floundering bodies disappear beneath the black water, and the waves cut furrows into the surface of the sea before filling them again.

The surface of the pond that revealed these scenes to me vanished, and was once again cloaked in darkness. Someone grabbed me by the scruff of the neck and dragged me away. I floated in the darkness like smoke.

Down below I saw the murky bottom of the container ship. I saw Xiang, and myself slumped beside her, and the middle-aged woman who no longer had the strength to stand. Then I saw each man in turn. I also saw other people stuffed in the spaces between the other rows of containers. Several people pulled food from a cloth bundle and ate it. One of the men violently shoved someone who was trying to steal a peek. Three men fumbled their way toward one woman. She tried to push them away and then fell to the floor. Her trousers and knickers were pulled down at the same time, and I saw the men take turns on top of her.

Xiang crawled in search of water. She lifted the bucket above her head and opened her mouth wide, but not a single drop came out. Someone reached a hand toward me in the dark. Xiang shouted. The men stepped back in surprise, and from the exterior corridor two crewmen charged in. They kicked Xiang without mercy. Then they looked around and dragged out the young men. One of the crewmen brought out a small club. He beat the young men over the head and on the spine. The beating didn't stop until the men were flat on the ground.

After they'd each had a smoke, the crewmen dragged Xiang out to the corridor and pulled off her clothes. When she struggled and resisted, they thought nothing of punching her in the face over and over until she, too, went limp. More crewmen came down. They stood around chatting while Xiang's naked body was turned this way and that, and laid down as they did what they wanted with her. Then they left her passed out on the floor and disappeared.

Number Eight, the middle-aged woman, was slumped to one side and did not move: it became clear that she had died. The crewmen grumbled as they carried her out to the corridor by her arms and legs, up countless metal stairs to the landing, where they cursed and swore again and took a short break before going out to the darkened deck. Two men swung the body back and forth to the count of three and then let it go, into the black crests and white furrows.

—

When did that magpie get here?

The little featherbrain snatched up my spirit, my shadow-like spirit that sometimes stretched out long and sometimes shrank down small. It picked it up in its beak, flew into the air, and perched on a metal railing in the dark.

Way down below, like a scene from a play I watched as a child, I saw my body lying flat on the floor, dressed

126

in a traditional white blouse and black skirt. Evil spirits with concealed faces, dressed in black and half-hidden in the shadows, pulled off my clothes. From above, my body looked frail and gaunt. They took knives and carved me up. My spirit self shouted in alarm. They hacked off my arms, my legs, my head, and flung them to the side. Behind them, other dark spirits crowded around. They tossed my severed limbs back and forth. The dark spirits snickered raucously and began feasting on my flesh. The ones with my torso split my belly open, pulled out my intestines, my liver, my organs — and ate.

A storm of pain washed over me, and then all was silent. My spirit self watched as my flesh disappeared, and all that was left were the bones. The dark spirits snatched up my tibias and danced. They kept rhythm to the rattling of my shinbones. O fleeting life!

I fluttered in the passing breeze and dangled from the tip of a branch on the enormous zelkova tree. Did the magpie carry me here? The bird ferried over objects one by one and dumped them at the base of the tree. My leg bone, my arm bone, my little finger, the knucklebones of my toes all clattered together. At the end, something rolled and tumbled and came to a perfect stop at the top of the pile of bones: my skull. The magpie flew to the branch where my spirit hung and perched there. He rubbed his beak against the tree and squawked:

Live or die, live or die. No difference.

Grandmother appeared and shooed away the bird. Then she sat in front of my bones. She sorted through them while Chilsung picked up scattered shards in his mouth and brought them over. Grandmother fit my bones together and sang a slow song:

Throw her out, the little throwaway.
Cast her out, the little castaway.
Over the Mountain of Knives,
the Mountain of Fire,
past the Hell of Poison,
Hell of Cold,
Hell of Water,
Hell of Earth,
through the sufferings
of eighty-four thousand hells,
all the way to the ends of the Earth
where the sun sets in the western sky.
What new hell awaits you here?
Bitter souls, hungry souls,
souls burdened even in death,
endless and innumerable.
Return to life! Return!

My spirit felt as if it was being sucked down off the branch. It swirled around in the air, circling my bones several times as if being coaxed back into place, and then I was in one piece again. New flesh grew. I couldn't stop touching my arms and legs and stomach, like a person who'd just recovered from a long illness.

Okay, okay, time for you two to go.

Grandmother gestured to Chilsung and me to go back over the dark river.

Grandma, where are you going?

This world is the liminal zone for those awaiting rebirth. I can't stay here. I'll come find you in your dreams.

Grandma, Grandma! Don't leave me!

Grandmother vanished like a bubble popping. Chilsung and I stood together next to the river. I walked back and forth through the grass, searching for the bridge that was no longer there, when I finally remembered the last remaining peony in my pocket. I took it out and threw it into the river as hard as I could. A five-coloured rainbow appeared and arced over the water. Chilsung ran ahead of me, tail wagging, and we crossed over together. The river was calm; I did not hear any shrieks this time. When I got to the other side and looked behind me, all I saw was blackness. But under my feet, the path forked. Chilsung hung back and waited for me to choose. I thought about how Grandmother had warned me to avoid the blue and yellow paths and follow only the white path. I placed my foot on the white path that glowed like the moon was shining down on it. Only then did Chilsung race ahead of me. When the path ended, and I was standing in front of another dark wall, Chilsung took several steps back, stared at me, and slowly wagged his tail. I knew this was goodbye again. I heard his voice inside my head.

No matter where you are, I'll come find you.

I put my hand out to try to pet him, but he, too, suddenly vanished.

SEVEN

When I arrived in that far-off distant land, I was sixteen years old, and it was autumn.

Our paths split there. I wouldn't find out until more than a year later that Xiang had stayed in the house we were taken to on our first night in London. I had no memory at all of how we got there, probably on account of the strange talent I had for separating my spirit from my body. Even the ten days or more that we spent inside a shipping container while the ship sat in the harbour, waiting to clear customs and be unloaded, came to me as nothing more than a vague dream when Xiang told me about it later — after she herself had recovered, of course. She was no longer as talkative as she used to be. She put it to me simply:

'We almost died.'

'How?'

'Not enough air.'

She told me we'd managed to find air by lying flat against the floor of the double-plated container and pressing our mouths to coin-sized holes drilled into the base. I remembered what happened once we were off the boat. We were driven for hours in the middle of the night and dropped off on some London street in front of a tiny warehouse. The men were taken away first.

The following day, Xiang and I were led to a house in a back alley not too far away in Chinatown. We went up a narrow stairway and down a hallway lined with rooms on both sides. The doors opened, and big women with blonde and brown hair peeked out. We were guided all the way down the hallway and into a room with a sofa. A white woman who was so overweight that she huffed and puffed with each breath came into the room and said something in English. The man who'd brought us there told us to strip. The three of us — Xiang, the woman who'd been on the boat with us, and I — hesitated, then slowly began to take off our clothes. The man cursed and yelled at us to move faster. I covered my chest with my arms and hunched over. The fat woman yanked my arms open and regarded my flat chest for a moment before sniggering at me. Xiang and the other woman stayed behind while I was taken alone to another location.

They took me to a small alley behind a street lined with Chinese restaurants. Waiting for us at the back door of a place called Shanghai Chinese Restaurant was Uncle Lou, the head chef. He took one look at me and shooed me inside. He called out someone's name and told her to take me upstairs and get me showered and changed.

For the first couple of weeks, I didn't speak to anyone else who lived there. I ate all my meals alone in the prep room at the back of the kitchen. When the doors were locked at one a.m. and everyone else had gone home for the night, I was left behind to clean the kitchen and the front of the restaurant on my own. It usually took me until well after two a.m. to finish. Then I would cover the prep table in the back with a plastic sheet and sleep on top of it with only a single blanket.

Those were unbearable days. I never got more than a few hours of sleep all night, and I was on my feet working all day. My job in the prep room was to clean and chop the vegetables and wash and scrub the dirty dishes that never ever stopped coming. I would scrape off the leftover food, scrub the plates and bowls with dish soap and stack them neatly in the dryer, only to find more endless stacks making their way in. And when lunchtime ended, I had to clean the entire place front and back again, and get it ready for the dinner rush.

It was several months before I could manage simple conversations with the young employees who worked in the front, and finally saw the face of the man who had purchased me from the snakeheads.

The restaurant was closed for three days at Christmas when Uncle Lou showed up unexpectedly. He told me he was meeting someone there. He handed me a sandwich that had been pressed flat and grilled, and asked for the first time where I was from. I told him I was an ethnic Korean from China. Most of the people who worked there were from southern China, so as long as I said I was from the northeast, my accent wouldn't arouse any suspicion. Lou told me he had come to London illegally from Hong Kong on his own over twenty years earlier. He'd stowed away on a ship like the rest of us. Then he let out a long sigh and shook his head.

'I could never do that again. Took me eleven years just to get a residence card.'

He asked about my smuggling debts. I had no idea how much had been paid before I left China, or how much still had to be paid.

'What kind of work did you do in China?'

'Foot massage. But I didn't have a licence for it.'

'That licence would be useless to you here anyway.'

Uncle Lou told me there were others in the neighbourhood who employed people like me, people working to pay off their smuggling debts. He also said that the boss liked me. Based on what he'd seen of other people my age, my zest for life meant I'd have my debts paid off within a year or two of hard work.

'If I were you,' he added, 'I'd find work at a foot-massage shop. With tips, you'd be making a lot more per week.'

I shrank into myself and muttered in a small voice: 'I don't know if I'm allowed to change jobs as I please.'

'No, of course you're not.' He looked determined. 'As the boss is giving your wages directly to your creditors.'

That year, there were non-stop fireworks and firecrackers for a week all around London on account of the twentieth century coming to an end. Chinatown was relatively quiet, as everyone there observed Lunar New Year, but the restaurant was even busier than before with tourists and other out-of-town visitors. The quiet days returned after the first of January, and Uncle Lou started dropping by the prep room where I worked to have a smoke.

One day he said: 'If things go well, you'll be able to find a new place to work.' Uncle Lou had a Vietnamese neighbour who owned a nail salon. He had told her he would vouch for me, and suggested we visit the salon together when the restaurant was closed on Monday.

'You're young and you work hard, so there's hope for you, despite that stupid debt of yours. If you can make better wages, you'll pay it off within a year.'

I bowed deeply to him in gratitude. I thought about Uncle Salamander that day for the first time in a long while. It was as if he'd followed me to London to watch over me. Tears poured out of me. It had been so long since I'd felt overcome with emotion that I thought I'd used up all my tears. Uncle Lou held out a freshly laundered napkin for me to wipe my eyes with.

'I left a daughter behind in China years ago. She must be about your age now.'

That Monday, I left Chinatown for the first time since arriving and took the London Underground with Uncle Lou. I was so afraid of losing him in the crowd that I clung to the hem of his shirt each time we got on and off the train. I learned later that the name of the station we were going to, and the neighbourhood it was in, was 'Elephant and Castle'. We went out one of the exits, crossed several streets in front of the plaza and arrived at the Tongking Nail Salon. Like the restaurant we worked at, it appeared to be open all week except Mondays. My life had been limited to Chinatown, where almost everyone was East Asian and resembled each other; there was the occasional white tourist, but they were just passing through. But as I walked around Elephant and Castle, I saw all kinds and colours of people. I saw yellow faces, brown faces, black faces, and occasionally a few white faces — but they weren't British; they blended in well enough, but were actually construction workers from Poland and the Czech Republic. Everyone else was a person of colour, like us.

Uncle Lou tapped on the glass door of the empty nail salon. A man who'd been reading a newspaper in one of the massage chairs looked up, smiled, and came over to unlatch the door. He was small and wiry, wore a white gown over his clothes, and looked Vietnamese. He and Uncle Lou spoke English to each other. I could tell from the way Lou gestured and glanced back at me that he was making an introduction, so I bowed and greeted the man. This was Uncle Tan, the owner of the salon.

'Let's show him what you can do,' Uncle Lou said.

Uncle Tan placed a stool in front of the chair and set his feet on it. I offered to start by washing his feet first, but Lou replied that Uncle Tan only needed a preview.

I squatted down before Tan's thin, bony feet and closed my eyes for a moment. The paths he had walked came to me faintly at first, but then they stood out clearly and began to move past, scene by scene. A cement wall collapsed, and a horde of people surged through the break. I spotted Tan amid the crowd, dressed in a black leather jacket. Then I saw him crossing hills and fields in another country, then taking a boat down a canal.

'Kid, what're you doing?' Lou asked. 'Why haven't you started yet?'

I opened my eyes.

'This man came from a place with a broken wall. He climbed over a mountain and rode a boat.'

135

Uncle Lou translated, and their eyes widened.

'How do you know that?' Lou asked. 'Tan was in East Germany when the wall came down. Then he crossed the border into the Netherlands and lived in Amsterdam for several years.'

I nodded.

'Whenever I look at someone's feet, I can tell where they've been.'

I added that I could also tell whether they were sick or healthy. I began to rub Uncle Tan's feet. A red aura appeared to me around the meridian point at the centre of the bottom of his foot. When I pressed it, he let out a low sigh. I repeated the eight steps of the basic foot massage and massaged about half the acupressure points of the foot, which numbered more than one hundred.

'Your kidneys are unhealthy,' I said, wiping the beads of sweat from my forehead.

When Uncle Lou translated this, Tan shook his head and whistled. He stood up, took a ten-pound note from his trouser pocket and handed it to me.

'Take it. You did good work.'

Lou translated again. I bowed my head in gratitude and took the money. The two of them spoke for a long time. On the way back, Lou told me: 'He wants to hire you. Didn't I say you have talent?'

I began working at Tongking the very next week. Uncle Tan had me move in with a Bangladeshi woman who worked at the salon. Luna was three years older than me. She was only twenty, but had already had two kids. She'd married at sixteen and become pregnant right away, but after a few years, she left her husband and came to London. After she and I became friends, she showed me the scars on her back and thighs from where her husband had beat her.

As usual, luck was on my side. There were low-income, high-rise apartment buildings near the salon that were subsidised by the district office, but the conditions were terrible. Most of the flats were tiny and consisted of only a single room, or a room with a living room-slash-kitchenette. Children ran wild through the hallways, and the flats were crammed with up to ten people each. Most of the tenants were immigrants, but Luna lived on a street lined with row houses in a borough called Lambeth. It was just as poor as the other neighbourhood, but quieter and safer. The whitewashed brick buildings, which were so old I had no idea when they'd been built, looked clean from the outside. Each row house was three stories with a half-basement; it was in one of these half-basements that I came to live with Luna. A flight of stairs at the entrance of the building led down to her flat, but our kitchen opened onto a small terrace so it didn't feel that much like being underground.

As this place became my new world, I should probably introduce the other people who lived there. As soon as you came down the stairs, you saw a narrow hallway with doors on each side facing each other. Each flat was a long rectangle divided into a kitchen and a room that served as both bedroom and living room. A Nigerian couple lived across from us. The husband worked at a gas station, and the wife was a part-time housekeeper.

The first-floor flat on the right was occupied by a

Chinese cook and a Filipino janitor, who were roommates like Luna and me. The flat on the left had a Sri Lankan family living in it. They ran a small restaurant nearby. Up on the second floor was a Polish family. The husband did home repairs and ran seasonal work teams staffed with labourers from his hometown. His wife and daughter worked together as shop assistants. Living in the flat to the left of theirs was Abdul, an elderly man from Pakistan. His was the only name I remembered, because Luna had taken me to meet him right after I moved in.

Grandfather Abdul, who managed the units in our building, wore a traditional tunic that buttoned all the way up to his throat and came down to his knees. His beard was white, and his brown skin looked as though it had been darkened by the sun. When Luna introduced me to him, he prepared tea for us that smelled like mint. He was always reading from a thick book, his reading glasses perched low on his nose. Only later, after I'd picked up some English and was able to converse with him, did I learn that it was the book of Islamic scripture, the Qur'an.

The landlord, a forty-something Indian man, came by on occasion to visit Grandfather Abdul. He was always sharply dressed in a suit and tie, and had never once spoken to me or even so much as greeted me. The first time I bumped into him out front, I thought he was from the immigration office and nearly turned and ran. Grandfather Abdul always called him 'Mr Azad', even though the landlord looked young enough to be his son.

Oh, I almost forgot about the people who lived on the third floor. I'd thought that the Chinese chef, the Filipino janitor, and I were the only East Asian faces in the building, but up on the third floor on the right-hand side was a married couple from Thailand who were there as students. An elderly Bulgarian couple lived across from them. I think that about covers it as far as our building and my world were concerned. My days mostly followed the same pattern: I woke up at seven, prepared a simple breakfast to eat with Luna, went to English classes that started at nine and studied for three hours, ate a sandwich for lunch at the English school's snack bar or somewhere else nearby, and then headed over to Tongking, where I worked from one in the afternoon to nine o'clock at night. The place where I studied English was referred to as a 'visa school': people attended in order to secure a residence visa. It cost half of what the other schools charged, and most of the students were women working in bars or similar types of establishments. They would show up only half the time, and barely paid attention when they did. Attendance would suddenly skyrocket at the beginning of the week that classes were being assigned, and then it would peter out again. There were a few students who showed up every day without fail, but the teachers didn't make much of an effort.

At the salon where I worked, Uncle Tan and four of the women who'd learned nail art gave manicures and pedicures to customers, while I was there to give them foot massages either during or after their treatments. Customers who were short on time turned down the massages, but we started to get more and more who came back just for one, after having had a taste of it. On Uncle Tan's recommendation, I taught Luna how to give foot massages as well. It only made sense, as she was helping me to study English. Being roommates with Luna, who'd grown up in England, helped me to pick up the language much faster than when I was in China. Talking to customers all afternoon in the salon was also a big help.

One day, I left work first and arrived home only to realise that I'd forgotten to get the key from Luna. I rummaged through my bag and stamped my feet in frustration outside our door; there was nothing else to do but run back up to the first-floor entrance and ring Grandfather Abdul's doorbell. His voice came over the intercom, asking: 'Who's there?' I told him I was Bari from the basement, and that I'd forgotten my key. The door opened and I headed up the stairs. He was standing outside his door, watching me from over his reading glasses.

'Come on in,' he said.

When I stepped inside, I saw a man sitting in the living room. He stood up to greet me. He was very tall, almost as tall as the floor lamp shining up at the ceiling, but it wasn't just his height that was imposing. He also had broad shoulders and long arms. His curly hair was cropped short, and his large eyes were open wide in his brown face, the whites showing around the irises. At first I was too afraid to look directly at him. Later I found out that he'd played cricket when he was in his teens, at school.

'Rest here for a bit,' Grandfather Abdul said. 'When Luna gets home, she can let you in, right?'

'Yes. Thank you, sir.'

'You probably haven't eaten yet. Would you like a piece of pie?'

I was too afraid to sit down in front of the strange giant, so I stood there timidly and said: 'No, thank you.'

'Oh, this is my grandson, Ali.'

Ali stooped from the waist and extended his big bear paw of a hand to me.

'Pleasure to meet you.'

His voice was deep and husky. I put my hand out too. To my surprise and relief, Ali grasped the tips of my fingers lightly and then quickly released them. I sat across from him. Each time our eyes met, he grinned at me. His smile, with those big, even teeth of his, was so friendly that I relaxed and began to smile back.

'What kind of work do you do?' Ali asked.

'I work at a nail salon. What about you?'

Grandfather Abdul placed a slice of the pie that he'd warmed in the oven on a plate and set it in front of me.

'Ali drives a minicab,' he said.

I didn't know what that meant, so they explained that it was not an officially licensed taxi, but a private car hire. Ali was paid by the hour to drive one of several cars owned by the person who ran the company. He didn't own his own cab, and he wasn't officially employed. Ali mostly worked the night shift. I didn't know what to say about that, so I asked him: 'You're not working tonight?'

Ali glanced at his grandfather before saying: 'It's his birthday tomorrow.'

Grandfather Abdul, who was standing at the sink, let out a hearty laugh.

'I was born so long ago that I can't even remember the date anymore, but he always remembers for me.'

'Actually, I forgot too. Mum called to remind me,' Ali said with a laugh.

I tucked into the pie and had a cup of tea afterward as well.

'Ali's parents live in Leeds,' Grandfather Abdul said. 'I keep telling him to move in with me, but he's stubborn.'

Ali just laughed and didn't say anything back.

'You and Luna should come back tomorrow and eat dinner with us. Have you ever had Punjabi food?'

'No, I haven't. I'll let her know.'

'I would invite the other neighbours, but they all live with their families.'

He seemed to feel apologetic about the fact that he was only inviting the two of us. I'd wanted to get to know him better for a while, as he'd made such a nice impression on me, and here I was getting to know his grandson as well.

The following day, as luck would have it, Luna and I were able to leave work an hour earlier than usual; as the salon was closed the day after, Uncle Tan didn't object to our leaving early. Luna and I stopped at a takeaway place and bought some Malaysian Chinese food. She warned me that Muslims didn't eat pork, and selected shrimp and chicken dishes as well as vegetable-fried rice made with mushrooms and bamboo shoots. When we got to the apartment building and started walking up the stairs, the smell of cooking wafted down the hall. There were so many different nationalities under one roof that whenever a holiday evening rolled around, the building was filled with all kinds of food smells, though no one ever complained.

We rang the bell, and Grandfather Abdul opened the

door. He was wearing his usual long tunic over a pair of *shalwar* trousers. Luna and I each greeted him by saying, 'Happy birthday, Grandfather!' Ali smiled at us; he was standing at the kitchen sink. The table was already set with big plates stacked with lamb kebabs and chicken curry with green chillies. When we filled some empty plates with the takeaway food we'd brought, Grandfather Abdul's small table was completely full.

Ali prepared ready-made *chapatti* by heating it in a dry frying pan. Ali placed the bread in a basket, and the four of us sat around the table. Grandfather Abdul poured *chai* for everyone. As Muslims didn't drink alcohol, it seemed we would have to skip the birthday toasts. Before we began eating, Grandfather Abdul said a prayer that began with *'Bismillah'*. Ali prayed with him. We were so hungry that we ate and ate.

Ali's parents and younger sister lived in northern England, in Leeds. His father moved to Britain from Pakistan after he turned five, and had grown up in this building, but moved to Leeds for work when he turned twenty. Grandfather Abdul said that back in his home country everyone from grandfather to grandson and grandson's wife lived under the same roof; he added that it was the only way to maintain close family ties. After dinner we had coffee and sweet almond cookies. I was completely stuffed. Ali blinked his big eyes at me, his eyelashes sweeping up and down, as he told his grandfather: 'I'll be right back. I'm going to walk Bari home.'

Grandfather Abdul smiled and didn't say anything. Luna looked at me and opened her hands wide, as if to say she was at a loss for words. Ali snuck a paper bag out from under the sink and hid it beneath his shirt. We all said goodbye to Grandfather Abdul and headed down to the basement. The moment we stepped inside our flat, Ali put his right hand to his chest, bowed his head, and apologised.

'I can't smoke or drink in front of my grandfather,' he explained.

Luna said to me: 'I don't care if you don't care.'

'I don't care,' I said.

Ali poured us a little of the whisky he'd brought. Then he lit up a long Pakistani cigarette made with whole-leaf tobacco. He looked happy as he gulped down the whisky. Luna drank too, grimacing as she did so, and I tried a sip only to break into a coughing fit. Ali seemed completely different away from his grandfather.

'I didn't think I'd make it through dinner!' he exclaimed. 'I can't drink so much as a single drop of beer around him.'

Luna sipped the whisky and said sarcastically: 'It's better to be British. Muslims have too many things they're not allowed to do.'

'I *am* British,' Ali said.

Luna snorted.

'The asshole who beat me every day was born here too,' she said. 'I don't care if someone is Hindu or Muslim or whatever. I don't trust anyone.'

Ali didn't look offended. He poured himself another glass, but this time he sipped it rather than downing it all at once.

'My father and grandfather don't get along. But my mum worries about him a lot.'

'Don't you visit him often?' I asked.

Ali cocked his head to one side.

'Maybe about twice a month,' he said. 'I prefer living by myself, but whenever I do come to visit, I feel more relaxed afterward for some reason.'

Luna took out a pack of cards and we played at the table. I don't know if Ali lost on purpose or if he just had bad luck, but we won about thirty pounds from him. Luna and I rejoiced at having earned some fun money for the weekend. We played until late into the night, and when it was time for Ali to leave I followed him to the door so I could lock it behind him. At the door, he whispered to me:

'You have the day off tomorrow, right?'

'Yes.'

'Would you like to take a drive out of the city with me?'

Clueless as to Ali's feelings for me, I turned and shouted to Luna: 'Ali wants to hang out with us tomorrow!'

Ali shook his head, and Luna barked with laughter.

'Hey stupid, he's asking *you* out! Why would I want to be a third wheel?'

Finally I understood and shut the door in his face. I looked through the peephole. Ali stood there for a while and then slowly turned and went back up the stairs.

'You've got an admirer,' Luna said teasingly. 'This is where ladies like us have to be careful.'

'What're you talking about?'

'That big elephant of a man is coming after you!'

Ever since I'd had that vision where my spirit split from my body, I'd stopped fearing any man. Uncle Lou, the chef from Shanghai Chinese Restaurant, had guessed what happened to me, but Uncle Tan and the employees of Tongking probably had no idea. I was still just a poor little thing. I wasn't surprised when my first period started so late, back when I was working at the restaurant. Xiang had warned me early on about a lot of things I would need to know, and as far as I was concerned I'd already become a woman long before that.

I did not take that drive with Ali to the countryside, but I did come to think of him differently, with those big eyes and that big body of his. Men and women are not the same, of course, but Grandfather Abdul's warm and caring nature made me feel that my grandmother had been reborn and returned to me. Ali, on the other hand, was just an oversized, immature boy — and maybe that was why I was so comfortable with him from the get-go.

EIGHT

I had been working at Tongking for several months before Auntie Sarah, one of the salon's regulars, requested a foot massage. At first she kept glancing over and watching as I massaged the feet of a customer sprawled out on the reclining salon chair, but as soon as I was done she motioned to me with her chin and waved me over.

'I'll have one of those,' she said.

She was an attractive, dark-skinned woman with a high nose and big eyes, and had probably been a great beauty in her younger days. I found out later that she was mixed — Sri Lankan and white. She practised Christianity, like her English father.

As usual, I held her long, thin feet in my hands and closed my eyes for a moment. In my mind's eye I pictured the various twists and turns her life had taken, though none were violent: a white man walks out of a house while a woman holding a child leans against the door and cries. Another man appears; he's black. Then the woman, who is alone again, is working in a hospital. Her daughter, now a toddler, crawls between the other children in a nursery.

'Why haven't you started yet?'

At Auntie Sarah's urging, I began the massage. She looked exhausted. I put everything I had into kneading and tapping her feet, plucking the joints of the toes and applying acupressure. She soon fell asleep. I closed my eyes again and pictured her as a grown woman, dating and breaking up with different men. Whenever a customer fell asleep we made a point of not disturbing her for a while, even after her session was complete.

Auntie Sarah always dressed well, wore expensive jewellery and tipped generously, so we regarded her as a wealthy woman completely out of our league. Whenever she came by, Tan treated her like royalty. But when I touched her feet, I realised that she wasn't all that different from the rest of us.

Luna and Auntie Sarah did not get along at all. Luna hated the way Auntie Sarah, despite being a fellow person of colour, looked down on her and treated her like a servant. But I made a point of being extra polite as I washed Auntie Sarah's feet, trimmed her toenails and cuticles and scraped the callused skin from her heels. When she woke, I served her warm tea and ended the session by massaging cream into her legs and feet and wrapping them with a warm towel. She tipped me ten pounds. Other customers usually only tipped us in change; at most you might receive a five-pound note.

As we began to get more customers looking for foot massages, Luna, who'd learned the basics from me, began giving them herself, along with a Vietnamese woman named Vinh who had quickly picked up the technique from watching me. Auntie Sarah became one of my regulars. She rarely spoke to any of us directly, but one day she asked Uncle Tan for a favour after paying her bill.

'I'd like to chat with the girl for a moment. Would that be okay? I'll pay for her time.'

'No problem, madam,' he said. 'You can talk to her as long as you want.'

Tan smiled at me and motioned with his chin for me to go with her. I followed her out of the shop. She looked around, her brow furrowed, and headed for a café across the street. She lit up a cigarette.

'Where are you from?' she asked.

I hesitated, then told her I was from China. She nodded.

'It doesn't matter where you're from as long as it's not Thailand.'

I had no idea what that meant, but just sat there quietly.

'I'd like to introduce you to someone. Naturally, I will speak with your employer about it, but let's just say I'm hiring you for a job. All you have to say is that you'll be working at my house. If you promise not to say anything stupid, I'll see to it that you earn some good money.'

'Yes, madam.'

Auntie Sarah puffed away on her cigarette, deep in thought for a moment.

'How's Wednesday?' she asked. 'If she likes you, she'll probably want to see you at least three times a week. I myself wouldn't mind having one of your massages every day if I could.'

'As long as our boss allows me to, I don't mind.'

'What's your name?'

I told her, and she told me her own. She also asked

149

whether or not I had any family, which neighbourhood I lived in, and how old I was. I answered all of her questions.

Then she said: 'This is the most important question ... Do you have a boyfriend?'

Later I thought it strange that Ali was the first person to come to mind when she asked me that; but all I said was: 'I don't even have any female friends, other than my roommate Luna, let alone a boyfriend.'

'Good! Well, except for that brat Luna.'

———

Auntie Sarah and Uncle Tan reached an agreement: I was allowed to leave the salon every Wednesday. Auntie Sarah drove me there herself the first day. As the only places I'd been were Piccadilly Circus near Chinatown and Elephant and Castle, I had no idea where she was taking me. It turned out to be a dazzling white three-storey mansion near Holland Park in Kensington. The garden was so lush with trees that from the outside only a few windows were visible. Next to the front door was a set of stairs that led down to the basement. Auntie Sarah took me downstairs first, past a kitchen, laundry room, and maids' quarters, then back up to the ground floor where we crossed a large reception hall, and up further to the second floor. There, in the second-floor living room, I met Lady Emily for the first time. She was a fifty-something woman with a dreamy look in her eyes, as if she'd just awoken from a nap. I knew nothing about the rich, the bluebloods of this country, but what I did catch on to right away was the fact that, aside from Lady Emily

150

herself, every person in that house existed to serve a master or mistress. (I never did catch so much as a glimpse of the master of the house.) Lady Emily wore a white dress and sat at a table talking on the phone while Auntie Sarah and I stood in the doorway and waited a long time for her to finish. Finally she set the receiver down and stared at us.

'Madam, the masseuse has arrived,' Auntie Sarah said politely.

Lady Emily shuffled through some mail and receipts that were sitting on the table and asked absent-mindedly: 'You say she's Chinese?'

'Yes, madam.'

'Well, you've really talked her up. Let's see how good she is.'

'I'll prepare the things.'

We went into the bedroom. Next to a *chaise longue*, Auntie Sarah set out some towels and a basin for the footbath, and prepared the herbal oils. She whispered to me: 'This is your job next time.'

Lady Emily entered and lay down at an angle on the *chaise*. I placed her feet in the warm water and slowly massaged her calf muscles. Then I dried her feet with a towel, warmed some herbal oil between my hands, and gently massaged her feet. I began with long strokes from heel to toe, kneading the entire sole of the foot. Then I closed my eyes and opened my mind to her.

A dark, cloud-like *something* was wrapped around her. I saw her leaving a villa in the middle of a huge forest with her husband. It was not in England. The scene changed, and I saw a small Southeast Asian woman standing next to her husband.

Lady Emily's face was smudged with tears as she argued with him. Everything looked like an out-of-focus photograph; only Lady Emily's face stood out clearly. What was that dark cloud? Another image began to take shape. Black women and children lay slumped in front of a clay house.

'Girl, what are you doing?'

I opened my eyes. Lady Emily was looking down at me pointedly.

'I was just concerned about your health,' I stammered.

'You're doing some kind of spell, aren't you? I could feel it at once.'

I didn't know how to tell her about my special abilities, but I sensed she might share the same gift. I pretended not to understand her question.

'All I did was close my eyes and try to sense whether you're ill or not.'

'There's more to it, isn't there?' Lady Emily asked, her head cocked to one side. 'Let me guess. You're some kind of shaman?'

I decided to come clean.

'I don't really know myself. I just know that I can tell things about people from touching their feet.'

'You said you're Chinese. What religion are you?'

'I don't follow any religion, madam.'

'Very well. Have you figured out what's wrong with me?'

I examined her feet as I rubbed them. A red aura appeared over the cushiony flesh at the base of her first two toes. Her ankle also glowed dark red.

'You might have a weak heart, and I think your knees bother you.'

Lady Emily studied my face, intrigued.

'You saw my past too, didn't you?'

I had no choice but to tell her what I saw.

'There were trees all the way to the horizon, and you were leaving a large stone house with rows of pillars.'

'That's right! That was Johannesburg! How did you know?'

'A small woman was standing next to the master of the house. I think that's why you two were arguing.'

Lady Emily clasped her hands in front of her chest in shock. She took several long breaths. Her eyes were turning red. It took her a while to calm her breathing. Then she dropped her hands.

'It's a good thing you're not Thai,' she said.

I decided not to mention the dark cloud yet, or the piled-up bodies of black women and children. Lady Emily lay back on the *chaise* and gestured.

'You may massage me now.'

I began by applying pressure with my thumbs and stroking with the flat of my hands, progressing from the bottoms of her feet to the tops, then to the toes, heels, and finally her calves. I massaged every acupressure point I knew. At some point she fell asleep. I ended the session by wrapping her feet in another warm towel, then massaging cream into her legs and feet. As I always did with clients, I crept out of the room to avoid waking her. Auntie Sarah was reading a magazine in the living room. She stood up when she saw me.

'Done?'

'Yes, madam. Lady Emily is asleep.'

'That's good. I guess it's my turn now.'

We went down to the maids' quarters in the basement. Auntie Sarah was in charge of the maids, which put her on nearly equal footing with the butler, an Indian man. She sat down on a sofa with her legs outstretched while one of the maids brought a towel and a basin filled with warm water. In the middle of the massage, a voice came over the intercom saying that Lady Emily was looking for her. Auntie Sarah quickly dried her feet and went upstairs. She came back shortly, her face aglow.

'She was really happy with you,' she said. 'She wants you to come back tomorrow.'

Auntie Sarah told me she would drive me back, but added: 'Here is the address. Can you find your way back here on your own tomorrow? All you have to do is ring the bell at the door we used earlier.'

On the way to Elephant and Castle, she said: 'By the way, Lady Emily says you have an unusual talent?'

I had to repeat the brief conversation I'd had with Lady Emily.

'That's extraordinary!' She shook her head. 'I can't believe you saw the Johannesburg estate. Her family lived in South Africa for generations.'

When I also told her about the small Southeast Asian woman, and how agitated Lady Emily had become, Auntie Sarah's voice turned angry.

'You said something stupid after all! That Thai bitch is the reason her husband is living in Brighton and not here. How embarrassing for her.'

She mumbled to herself for a bit, then whipped her head

around to look at me; something had just occurred to her.

'That means you saw something when you touched my feet, too!'

I didn't answer, but she immediately chuckled to herself as if to say there was no use worrying about that now.

'I guess you saw all my dreadful ex-boyfriends.'

I debated whether or not to keep quiet, but then decided to say something in order to hold her attention a little bit longer.

'I saw your white father, and the black man your mother met when she was working at the hospital.'

'Oh my!' Auntie Sarah's hands slipped on the steering wheel, and the car swerved. 'You're really something, kid!'

I didn't tell her about the form that looked like a dark cloud wrapped around Lady Emily, or the bodies. When the car pulled up in front of Tongking, she handed me an envelope. I got out of the car and looked inside: there was far more in there than just my hourly fee. If I kept working at that rate, I would be able to pay off my debts in Chinatown within six months. For the first time I felt my heart grow lighter. I gave the money for my hourly fee to Uncle Tan and kept the rest. He looked satisfied to have such a wealthy regular who would provide a fixed income for the salon.

The following week, I took the Underground to the mansion on my own, address in hand. I was so scared that my heart nearly beat out of my chest, but at the same time I was happy that I had the freedom to go anywhere now.

By the time I had made the two station transfers, walked down the side street next to Holland Park, and arrived at the house in Kensington, I was ten minutes late. I went

155

downstairs and rang the bell. Auntie Sarah's face appeared.

'I was worried you wouldn't find it,' she said.

'I took the wrong train and had to make a different transfer.'

'Lady Emily's waiting for you. She's already asked me twice why you're not here yet.'

Auntie Sarah led me up to the living room on the second floor. Lady Emily was resting on the sofa, wearing a sky-blue silk Chinese gown.

'Yes, come in,' Lady Emily said in a drowsy voice.

Auntie Sarah gave me a nod and then vanished.

'Would you like a cup of tea?' Lady Emily asked. 'We don't have to start with the massage today.' She spooned some dark tea into a porcelain pot that was ready on the table.

'Is that black tea?' I asked.

'No, it's made from medicinal herbs. It'll relax you and make you feel better.'

I took a hesitant sip. There was no flavour at all, but it smelled like dried leaves and earth. I followed Lady Emily into the bedroom; she had me recline on the *chaise* while she lay down on the bed.

'Let's converse, Bari. You'll know what to do.'

I felt my back start to rise and fall, as if I were bobbing on the ocean, and then my body went slack and I felt like I was floating down a river. From between my fluttering eyelids, which insisted on closing, I caught a glimpse of someone standing over Lady Emily's bed. It looked like an older black woman wearing a heavy brown cloak made from a rough material.

'There's someone behind you,' I said. 'A black woman.'

Lady Emily was not startled at all.

'Yes,' she whispered. 'That must be my nanny, Becky. She watches over me.'

I tried to sit up in order to greet Becky, but for some reason my arms and legs would not obey. Lady Emily's quiet voice reached my ears.

'Go to sleep, child. Go to sleep.'

—

I stand in a field with dry grass up to my waist. The setting sun looks like a deliciously ripe persimmon. It turns the whole sky a deep, orangey red. A slow rhythm, like distant drumming, vibrates in my ears. I can't tell whether or not it is my own heartbeat that I am hearing.

At the centre of the field, enormous stone mountains tower up out of the earth and seem to brush against the sky. The further I walk into the mountains, the more they resemble two palms opening. At the centre I see a large pit, like the mouth of some giant creature, gaping open in the middle of a wide clearing. The bottom of the pit is drilled here and there with dark holes that go so far down I cannot tell where they end. Black men, seemingly thousands of them, fill burlap sacks with stones dug from the sides and bottom of the pit with pickaxes and shovels. They haul the stones up rope ladders and march up the winding ledge that leads out of the pit, carrying their heavy loads.

To one side of the clearing, I see structures built from wooden planks, thatched roofs, and white canvas awnings.

White men sit in a circle beneath one of the awnings. One wears a white shirt and hat and has a moustache. I see soldiers in uniform.

I wander around inside the image. A rope ladder breaks and dozens of men are sent tumbling to the bottom of the pit. A gun goes off, and more shots follow sporadically. Then everything goes silent. The soldiers walk over to the fallen and inspect them.

I walk back to the field. The field is blanketed in the same black, fog-like shapes that I saw in my home country, and the low whoosh of the wind never stops. The sky is dim, as if the sun is on the verge of either rising or setting, and it is just as quiet. Spots of light appear here and there. Smoke rises from the roofs of a burned village, and embers fly over the burned grass and reeds. Everywhere, dead bodies are picked at by vultures and crows. The ground is littered with weapons. Did a battle take place?

I see trees. Baobab trees with their roots sticking straight up toward the sky. Ash, oak, acacia, marula. All kinds of trees tower over me like fortress walls, and at the centre I see a light. I slip between the trees, sliding toward the light. Patches of colour — white, ochre, grey, blue — appear in the light. People are there, dressed in colourful fabrics. I take a closer look and see that they are nearly all female: grandmothers, mothers, young women. And children: grandsons, granddaughters, newborn babies. The light is coming from an enormous bonfire rising from a triangular stack of logs. No one speaks.

They know that I am watching. And I know they are not alive. As I walk toward the bonfire, they cover their faces and step back to clear a path. Standing before the fire is a woman. She's been waiting for me. When I am standing before her, I see that it's Becky. She wears a headband laden with crystal beads on top of a headscarf, and on her body she wears a black skirt and a rough, brown cloth around her shoulders. Ostrich-tail feathers are stuffed in the back of the headband like scattered clouds floating over her head.

You must be Bari, the one my baby girl Emily sent.

She plucks one of the ostrich feathers from the back of her head and sweeps it along the ground, which splits open as if during an earthquake, and the people who were scattered about all crowd in at once, turn to shadows, and seep into the earth like fog, filling the crevasse. A hand sticks up out of the fog, then two arms, followed by a white man's face. It's the man with the moustache whom I saw sitting under the tent earlier. Another pair of flailing arms emerges, followed by the upper body of the white-haired man in the dark-red military uniform. The murky fog is less like a gas and more like a sticky, muddy bog. The shadows pull the two white men back down as they scream and shout.

Let me go!

Get us out of here!

Suddenly the crack vanishes, and the earth closes up. The shadows have resumed their original forms and are sitting and standing under the trees. The bonfire blazes again. From the entrance to the forest where I came in earlier, Lady Emily walks toward me, dressed in the same blue silk gown as before. Her eyes are wet with tears. She pleads with Becky.

Please release them.

Becky's face is impassive.

It's not me, child. The souls of the dead won't let them go.

How can they be set free?

Ask Bari.

———

Even before Lady Emily could say anything, my eyes were wide open. I could see the crystal beads on the chandelier that hung from the ceiling. Though my head was still foggy, the objects in the room and the leaves on the trees outside the window were in sharp focus. But the colours were all yellowed and faded, like an old photograph. I remained quiet for a moment until the colours were restored.

'You're awake!' Lady Emily said. She stood up and staggered over to me. 'So, what did you see?'

I couldn't begin to describe all the visions I'd had.

'I saw hundreds, maybe thousands, of African men working in a mine. And I saw a lot of people die, too.'

'That would've been a gold mine.'

'I saw two men … One was middle-aged. The other, a soldier, looked like an old man …'

When I told her about the earth opening up and the two trapped inside the black smoke, she pressed her hands to her heart and lowered her head.

'Oh, you saw my father and grandfather.' She clasped my hand tightly. 'You're a powerful psychic!'

Because I'd sensed that she shared my powers, I asked her: 'What did you see?'

'I saw a long river. And a mountain on fire … And I

think I saw a boat floating through the pitch black.'

'Did you see my grandmother? Or a white dog named Chilsung?'

'I couldn't see that far.'

I'd gotten a clear look at Becky and remembered her face and clothing, so I told her about the village with the giant bonfire.

'Becky worked for my family since I was four years old,' Lady Emily said. 'I think what you saw might've been her hometown. She was a traditional healer. I was the only one who knew she was a shaman.'

Lady Emily looked around and then rummaged inside a drawer in her nightstand. She pulled out a small box covered in red velvet, opened the lid and showed me a leopard's tooth, some jewels, and the bone fragments that Becky had used to cast divinations. Then she carefully took out a small figurine carved from ebony. It was about the size of a finger, and depicted a slim, dark-skinned African man. The eyes were long and slanted and the mouth was closed, the corners drawn down in a grimace. From between the legs rose a long, sharp penis — the moment I saw it, my hands started shaking uncontrollably, and I could feel a wave of heat roll from the back of my neck all the way up to my cheeks. I grabbed the doll from Lady Emily, stuck it back in the box and shut the lid. My breathing slowly returned to normal.

'That's Becky's husband in the world beyond. It's a custom where she is from, for shamans to marry the dead.'

'I have to go.'

Lady Emily placed her hands on my shoulders and spoke to me even more kindly than Auntie Sarah had.

'Can you come for just two days next week?'

'Okay.'

I had expended so much energy and time on Lady Emily that day that I was unable to give Auntie Sarah a foot massage. I said goodbye to her and headed back to Tongking. On the way, I kept thinking about that ebony figurine. Each time I closed my eyes, I felt as if it had turned into a giant person, and was right in front of me on the subway. It looked like Ali, in fact: like Ali was naked and standing before me. The brakes screeched and people poured on and off the train. I had my head down and my eyes closed when I heard a deep voice above me.

'Bari! Where're you going?'

Shocked, I raised my head. It was none other than Ali, the giant, looking down at me and smiling, his shoulders stooped. My eyes unconsciously slipped down to his crotch. I was sure that long, sharp penis would be hanging there. My face turned bright red.

'I made a house call, but now I'm headed back to the salon,' I said.

'I'm headed to work, too.'

Ali got off at Elephant and Castle with me, and we had kebabs at a Turkish restaurant nearby.

I returned home late that night and lay down next to Luna, who was fast asleep — but I kept tossing and turning. I would doze off for a moment, only to jerk awake. My ears hummed with the memory of my grandmother telling me one of her old stories. It was the one about Princess Bari, which she'd shared with me on snowy nights in the dugout hut across the Tumen River.

'Grandma, continue the story,' I said. 'You said Princess Bari scrubbed clothes and cooked food and chopped wood and did all kinds of menial labour and travelled all the way to Hell. And she saved the souls who were suffering there and went through Hell herself and came all the way to the western sky.'

'Yes, yes, you remember it well. When she gets to the western sky, she is stopped by a *jangseung* — the wooden totem pole that stands guard at the border has come to life and is waiting for her. She loses a bet with him, and he recites the deal she must make: *three by three is nine*. She will have his babies and cook and clean for him for nine long years in exchange for the life-giving water. How do you suppose she met him in the first place? She avoided the blue and yellow paths and stuck to the white path, getting help along the way, but suddenly this giant, black totem pole of a man appears before her. *Aigo! Aigo!* What is she to do? If she falls into his clutches, all will be lost. She has to be clever and talk her way out.'

'Grandma, did Bari ask the totem pole how to get to the western sky?'

'Yes, yes, and the *jangseung* tells her: "There's no such place. You have to live with me. My grandfather didn't marry until the age of ninety-one, as he found no woman before that. I'm lucky to have met you, so now you must live with me." Bari keeps talking, trying to distract him as she edges away from him, but he throws her over his shoulder.'

I recited Princess Bari's lines: 'Hey! Put me down! We can walk together.'

'So they begin walking, her in front and him behind.

163

As they walk, he tells her he lives in an earthen cottage with a straw mat for a door. Then he says he lives in a big house with a grand, tiled roof. Finally he says: "Forget it, we'll just live in the first place we see." When they find it, it's more of a shack than a house. The door is just a flimsy straw mat. With the sun shining brightly down on Bari, it seems she will be stuck with him for good once they are married and spend their wedding night together, so she sets out a bowl of clear water in the courtyard, lets down her hair, and throws herself on the ground, kicking and keening.'

Then Grandmother mimicked the totem pole's voice: 'Ah! Why are you crying?'

I answered as Princess Bari: 'Today is the anniversary of my grandfather's death.'

'Bari stays up all night mourning. The next day, as evening approaches, she lets down her hair again, draws fresh water from the well, and falls to the ground, weeping and wailing.

'Why are you crying this time?'

My turn again: 'Today is the anniversary of my grandmother's death.'

'On the third night, she mourns again.

'Why are you crying this time?'

'Today is the anniversary of my father's death.'

'The next night she flops down and cries again, and he asks her what significance that day has.'

'Today is the anniversary of my mother's death.'

Grandmother grumbled comically: '"Huh! Did your whole family get the plague? How did they all die one after the other like that?" Then the fifth night rolls around …'

'Grandma, Princess Bari has to marry the totem now, right? What does she do?'

'Well, first, she pleads with him.'

I continued in Bari's voice: 'I beg you! If you and I are to marry, then we must pray to our ancestors first. But how can we do that in this messy, dusty old house? We'll hold memorial rites for our ancestors today, and cleanse and purify ourselves for the next three days. After that, we'll be ready for a proper wedding ceremony. I'll clean the house and sweep the floor, while you go chop us some firewood.'

'How dare you order me to chop wood?'

'Why aren't you leaving?'

'I'm afraid you'll run away.'

Grandmother took over Bari's part: '"You idiot! How on earth would I get away from you? I can't go anywhere, so hurry off. I'll tie this thread around my wrist and give the other end to you … so hurry off now." She begins cleaning the house and sweeping the floor. The stupid fool leaves. But he comes rushing back before it's even lunchtime, looking like he's fallen and cut and bruised himself along the way.'

'What happened to you?' I asked as Bari. 'Did you run into a bear? Did you run into a tiger?'

'No, my A-frame carrier kept tugging me this way and that, and I tripped and fell.'

'Ah, I have to move my hands back and forth to clean the house! What an idiot you are! Don't tie the thread around your carrier this time. Here, I'll draw you a picture of me instead. Take it with you and stick it to a tree. If it stays up, that means I'm still here. If it falls down, then it means I've run away. Be sure to use lots of glue and stick it on good.'

'So the *jangseung* takes the picture, and whenever he wants to see his future wife, he looks at it and smiles. He glues it to a pine tree, and it stays in place. Finally he can relax, knowing that she hasn't run away, and he goes to work chopping firewood.'

'Heaven brings the totem pole and Princess Bari together. Isn't that right, Grandma? And now they have to have children?'

At some point, while recalling, one by one, the stories my grandmother and I used to recite, I slipped into sleep.

NINE

One day, around the time I'd nearly paid off my smuggling debt — which means I must've been working at Tongking for about a year by then — Uncle Tan called me into the hallway at the back of the shop where the toilets were. I hadn't done anything wrong, but the grim look on his face made my heart race.

'Have you heard?' he asked. 'There's going to be a crackdown this week.'

'What kind of crackdown?'

'You don't have a visa or a work permit, do you?'

I looked down and thought about his question. Uncle Lou must have told him my story.

'Don't worry. I'm not going to fire you. The problem is that if we get caught, the worst that will happen to me is I'll be fined two thousand pounds and could lose my business licence, but you'll go to jail and get deported.'

Vinh, the Vietnamese girl who lived in a government-subsidised flat nearby, had gone home the night before to find that a joint squad of local police and UK Border Agency officers had arrived in several vans and were blocking the entrance to the apartment building. They searched door to door and took away a dozen illegal immigrants. Uncle Tan pulled some cash from his pocket and tried to hand it to me.

'I called up some friends,' he said. 'They said it looks like the shops in this area will be inspected this week. I need you to lie low until things have settled down. Shouldn't be more than a couple of weeks.'

I bowed several times and said: 'Thank you for warning me. And I don't need your money. I didn't earn it.'

'Take it. You can pay me back later.'

'As long as you'll hire me back, I'm really okay.'

I refused to take his money. When Luna saw me leaving early, she followed me out of the salon.

'Where are you going?' she asked. 'Is something wrong?'

'I'm fine. I'm just heading home early. I have a headache.'

She took my hand and shook it lightly.

'Okay, get some rest. Are you sure you're okay?'

I nodded, then turned and took my time walking back to our flat in Lambeth. By the time I got there the sun had already set, and the stairwell was dark. I groped my way downstairs. Suddenly the door across from ours swung open, and I saw a shadowy figure. It was the Nigerian woman who lived next to us.

'Oh! It's you,' she said. 'I was hoping it was …'

I wondered what she was doing in the dark. The lights were turned off inside her flat as well. The window that looked out onto the courtyard let in some light from outside, but it wasn't much.

'Is the power out?' I asked.

Finally she flicked the lights on, as if she'd simply forgotten about them. I took out my key and started to unlock my door, but when I saw she was still standing there, I said without thinking: 'Your husband isn't home yet?'

'No, I'm waiting for him,' she said.

I opened the door, but before I stepped inside, I glanced back again. She was leaning on the wall next to the door. I looked at her for a moment.

'Would you like some tea?' I asked.

I held the door open, and she slipped inside without a word. When I followed her in and closed the door, she collapsed against my shoulder and burst into tears. I was bewildered, but patted her on the back and asked what was wrong. She pulled away from me and sank onto the floor.

'My husband was arrested.'

I helped her up and led her over to the big, cushy armchair that Luna and I were always fighting over. Her face was streaked with tears.

'Someone who works at the petrol station with him called me. They took him because he doesn't have a work permit.'

My heart sank. So it was true!

'We went through so much to make it here …' she said. 'We have nowhere to go back to.'

I put a kettle of water on to boil and took out the teacups.

'He doesn't have a work permit, so he was paying a hundred pounds a week to borrow someone else's. But there's such a big age difference between him and the person he borrowed it from, that if they investigate him in person instead of just checking the paperwork, they'll catch him right away. You know, you get paid less if you don't have a permit — only half of what legal workers make, and sometimes as little as thirty percent. But if you borrow someone else's permit, you can make up to seventy percent of the regular wage.'

I poured her a cup of tea; she seemed to have calmed down already. She took a few deep breaths, and sipped her tea.

'If he's deported,' she muttered, 'I'll run away.'

She stared down at the floor.

'We left our children behind,' she said. 'All three of them. And we still haven't finished paying off the men who brought us here.'

I couldn't tell her that my situation was similar. I wasn't in a position to trust anyone yet. I'd been working hard to pay off my smuggling debt, not paying attention to anything else around me, but now I understood the seriousness of my situation. It occurred to me that I had to console her if I was also to console myself.

'Who knows?' I said. 'Maybe they'll let him go and he'll come back home …'

She shook her head weakly.

'That miracle already happened. There was a crackdown and he was sent to jail, but then there was a shift change and the new officer called names off of the list of work permit holders without bothering to check them against their photos. My husband told me a kindly old man who was among those being released took pity on him and had him take his place. Of course, they probably found out later what happened. Everything is the will of God.'

I kept my composure, but there was no doubt in my mind that danger was approaching. Her husband would be investigated; it would be discovered that he'd borrowed his work permit from someone else; they would find out where he lived; and his wife would be exposed too. The police might be there as early as the following morning. It was actually a good thing their children weren't living with them. She looked like she was out of her mind and giving up hope.

'Is there anywhere you can hide out for a few days?' I asked.

The gravity of her situation seemed to hit her all at once.

'*Ya Allah* … They could be here tomorrow!'

She pressed her hands to her chest and shook her head in panic. She seemed to freeze for a moment, then sprang up and opened the door.

'I'll call the woman I work for to see if I can stay with her. Who knows? Since I'm already looking after her house and children, she might prefer it that way …'

After she left, I paced nervously. I didn't know whether or not I should run away somewhere until things had calmed down. Soon, there was a knock at the door. I checked the peephole before opening it. It was the Nigerian woman again.

'She said I can stay with her for a few days. Luckily, her husband is away on business. She said to come to the house first to discuss it. Also, I called my husband's friend. He said he'll go to the detention centre tomorrow to try to get visiting hours with my husband.'

'That's good! I'm sure your husband will be back in no time.'

She threw her arms around me and murmured: 'Thank you. Why can't the rest of the world be like our building?'

After the door closed behind her, I paced some more and then came to a decision. I left the flat and went straight up to the second floor. I paused in front of Grandfather Abdul's door long enough to catch my breath, and tapped the bronze knocker. I heard him clear his throat, and then there he was. He lowered his reading glasses and peered down at me.

'Well, look who's here! Come in, Bari.'

I sat down across from him, but couldn't speak right away. I had my head down, deep in thought. He didn't rush me but simply waited, a soft smile on his face. Finally I explained why I'd come home early from work. I told him what had happened to the Nigerian couple across the hall from me. His smile vanished and he nodded, his brow furrowed.

'This country is very concerned with "public safety",' he said.

I didn't understand what he meant.

'It's the same everywhere you go. The powerful wealthy do whatever it takes to shore up their privilege. This crackdown is one example of that. I suppose you don't have a passport either, Bari?'

'Technically I do …'

'But of course, it's forged.'

Although I was still wary about trusting people, one thing I'd learned over the course of my travels was that if you needed help from a good person, you could best earn their trust by being honest with them. I told Grandfather Abdul where I was really from, and briefly described my journey through China and all the way here. He nodded now and then, and waited with a smile whenever I got worked up and had to pause to catch my breath. When I ended with my arrival in London, he sighed.

'Indeed. Let's consider what it is that keeps tearing the world apart. I came to London under very similar circumstances as you. I'm sure it's the same for the Nigerian couple. But I believe you're right, that you'd better be ready for the worst tomorrow. I don't think anyone else will be affected, though I worry about the young Filipino man on the first floor. By the way, have you had dinner yet? I can't imagine you've had a chance to eat.'

'Oh! Luna will be hungry when she gets home!'

'Hold on, now. I have some tandoori chicken. Let's eat that with *chapatti*. I'm tired of eating dinner alone. It would be nice if you could join me.' He put some marinated chicken in the oven and warmed up *chapattis* in a dry pan.

While we were eating, Grandfather Abdul said: 'You can stay here at night, but it's best if you go somewhere else during the day. I'll ask Ali to drive you somewhere.'

'But Ali works nights. Doesn't he need to sleep during the day?'

'It's fine. He won't be getting much work while this is going on. I'll just tell him to take a few days off.'

When I went downstairs, Luna was already home and washing rice for dinner. She stir-fried some meat and vegetables, then suddenly turned and pointed the wooden spatula at me.

'Where on earth have you been?' she yelled. 'I was so worried about you!'

I told her that I had gone to see Grandfather Abdul, and quickly filled her in on what Uncle Tan had told me at the nail salon and what happened to the Nigerian couple next door. She stopped cooking and turned off the stove.

'I don't know what all the fuss is about,' she said. 'This has been happening for years. My mother went through the same thing before I was born, and I dealt with it once as well. What do you think? That Immigration is going to come bust down our doors and search through every flat and check everyone's papers?'

'Luna, I need to pack a few things. You can tell them my clothes are yours. I'll leave some toiletries and a change of clothes in Grandfather Abdul's flat.'

Early the next morning, while Luna was still asleep, I packed a small bag and went upstairs to Grandfather Abdul's flat. He told me Ali would be there soon to pick me up, but I was still nervous; so he called Ali to make sure he was on the way. It turned out he wasn't even awake yet. Grandfather Abdul shouted at him.

'What are you still doing in bed? I just spoke to you about this last night! Get over here now!'

After he hung up, he paced around the flat with his hands clasped behind his back and kept returning to the window to look down at the street.

'He needs to get here before the Border Agency opens …'

Nearly an hour went by before Ali came thumping up the stairs and banged on the door.

'Why are you so late?' Grandfather Abdul said. 'Do you

want her to get arrested?'

Ali didn't seem to have grasped the situation. He grumbled sullenly: 'It took a while to get my friend to loan me his car. Doesn't she need a car if she's moving flats?'

'When did I say she's moving flats? I asked you to take some time off of work and take care of Bari for a few days!'

Ali caught my eye and grinned, his white teeth showing. Once we were out of the house and in the car, I felt more relaxed. I figured the Nigerian woman had also left home early to hide out at her housekeeping job. Grandfather Abdul said he'd warned the Filipino man, who worked as a hospital janitor. In any case, he had no desire to see any of his neighbours arrested or deported. He also didn't want Mr Azad, the landlord, to blame him when there was less rent to collect that month. The car that Ali had borrowed was a banger: the door was crushed in, and the bumper was nearly falling off.

'Where are we going?' I asked.

'I figure we'll go to my flat first,' Ali said as he slowly made his way out of my neighbourhood.

He probably didn't know the whole story, but I assumed that Grandfather Abdul had told him that I didn't have a work permit and was in danger of being deported.

'Don't worry,' he said. 'The minicab company I work for is also crawling with illegal immigrants. Some of them don't even have driver's licences.'

I didn't say anything at first, just sat there sullenly in the passenger's seat and muttered to myself: 'Why do we have to have borders, anyway?'

Ali lived in Shepherd's Bush, in West London, a

neighbourhood filled with people of different races, much like where I lived. It wasn't far from Holland Park, where Lady Emily lived. A single street separated the two neighbourhoods, yet they were completely different. The road split off into five directions, and was centred around an ugly, garbage-strewn park with patches of dirt showing through the grass. It reminded me of an unwashed puppy. Narrow alleys led back between the shop buildings along a curving market street. Ali's flat was located down one of the alleys, in a three-storey building with an unlit entrance.

It wasn't much, just a railroad flat the size of a small studio divided into two rooms. The front room had a double sink and a beat-up table with rickety legs and four chairs, and the back room had a bed pushed up against the wall. I don't know where he'd found it, but a metal chest of drawers, like something you'd see in an office, stood at the foot of the bed. I started to ask Ali why he didn't just live with his grandfather, but held back. Most young people probably wouldn't feel comfortable living with someone so much older.

That day Ali and I got to know each other a little better. I told him how I'd wound up in London, including how my family got split up, how I crossed the Tumen River and what had happened in China. Ali said he'd heard similar stories from his father and grandfather. Because he was born in Britain, he'd never seen where they were from. He had trouble pronouncing the name of their hometown.

'Srinagar. Have you heard of it?'

'No, never. Have you heard of Chongjin?'

'Chee-ung …?'

We spent the day in his room, and that evening Ali dropped me off at the flat while he went to work. When I walked in, Grandfather Abdul told me that a man and woman from the UK Border Agency had come by. They didn't search every flat, but they did ask him question after question about each of the residents. He showed them the tenant list and gave them everyone's name and occupation. Regarding the young Filipino man, he told them he was a previous tenant who had since moved. He said he didn't know where he was now. As for my flat, he told them Luna lived alone. In fact, Luna had rented the flat first; all she and I did was split the rent after I moved in. There was never any reason for my name to be added to the tenant list. They said they were going to inspect the Nigerian couple's flat, but Grandfather Abdul got up the nerve to stop them.

'I told them I could not unlock the door without the tenants' permission. I said if there were charges against them, then they could come back with a court warrant. As it is, they might still come back. It'll take a few more days to settle this.'

Grandfather Abdul offered me some *chapatti* and lamb. I tried to turn it down, but then offered instead to come back early the next evening and fix him a tasty dinner in exchange.

'So,' he said, as he sat down across from me. 'Is Ali taking good care of you?'

'Yes. But I don't understand why he lives alone.'

Grandfather Abdul laughed out loud.

'Neither do I! When I was his age, we all lived with extended family. After moving here, it took me several years

177

to get used to living alone. It was very hard on me when Ali's father married and got a job in Leeds. I was working in London, so I couldn't move there with them.'

Grandfather Abdul had worked in a hotel before he retired. He lived in the building for free in exchange for looking after Mr Azad's rental property. He told me the landlord worked in a bank and owned five such buildings.

'Poor Ali,' Grandfather Abdul said. 'He grew up sharing a room with several others. That's probably why he wants to live alone for now.' (Ali had told me bashfully that he had six brothers and sisters, so I understood at once what Grandfather Abdul meant.)

I spent the next three days hanging out in Ali's flat. I was following Grandfather Abdul's advice to lay low until the weekend. Luna relayed Uncle Tan's messages to me. Nothing had gone wrong at the salon, but I would need to keep my distance until the weekend. Then it would be okay for me to come back to work the following Tuesday. Luna also told me that Auntie Sarah had called several times: Lady Emily was looking for me.

—

Back then, whenever I felt lonely and whenever times were tough, I thought of my grandmother. I would mumble the old stories we used to recite to each other, first speaking in my voice and then switching to hers. I would hear Luna's light snores, and toss and turn in bed for a while before sending my spirit afloat. The more often I did this, the more clearly I was able to see my body lying below.

I would float up a little and look down at my body, curled on its side. I could see Luna's body too, and everything in the room. I would float higher as darkness closed around me and the white path appeared. It was always the same up to that point:

I take a few steps down the path, and Chilsung's white fur appears. As always, he is wagging his tail.

Chilsung-ah! I need to talk to Grandmother.

Okay, Bari. She's waiting for you.

Chilsung turns around and leads the way, glancing back at me now and then. I float behind him, along the dazzlingly white path. At the top of a hill shrouded in smoke-like wisps of fog, or maybe clouds, stands a tall, octagonal pavilion supported by stone steps. Wide, round pillars hold the heavy roof aloft. Grandmother waves at me from inside the pavilion.

Our little Bari! You've been through a lot, haven't you?

No, I'm okay.

It's a wonder you've made it this far. But there's still a long way to go. Look down there.

Grandmother stands at the railing and points. The white cloud-like things part, and just visible below are fields and mountains and rivers and a city.

Where is that?

That's where you live. You must have met people from all over the world by now.

Yes, all kinds of people.

Bari, have you figured it out yet? I tried to warn you when I was telling you those old stories. I told you the path you're on would bring you to a great many people who would ask for your help. And they'll keep asking why they must suffer.

Yes, and you told me that Princess Bari travelled to the otherworld to find out.

That's right, which means you need to be ready with an answer.

I won't know that until I've been to the otherworld.

Once you've been there, you'll be able to help all of them.

Even though we speak different languages and look different and come from different places?

Grandmother smiles, her wrinkles squeezing together.

Of course. The world and every person in it — we're all the same. We're all lacking and sick and stupid and greedy.

I feel for them, I say.

Bari, I'm so proud of you! It's when you learn to empathise that the answer comes to you.

Grandmother waves her hand again, and the cloud-like things blanket the pavilion in white.

Now you'll marry the jangseung. *You'll have to search for the life-giving water while you're living with him.*

Grandma, do other people have ancestral spirits like me?

Of course. They're everywhere. All souls are washed from muddy to clean. I have to go now. It's time for you to go, too.

I fly out of the pavilion like a puff of smoke on the breeze. The clouds or fog surround me, and there is Chilsung again, wagging his tail on the path that I came down earlier. No sooner am I back, floating near the ceiling of my bedroom and looking down at myself, than my spirit returns to my body and my eyes open. The dark branches of trees are visible through the window.

—

I think it was the afternoon of my third day at Ali's flat. We were sitting at the table when he suddenly leaned over and kissed me. I wiped my mouth with the back of my hand, and he laughed and copied me. He wouldn't stop snickering. I didn't know what was so funny about it.

'What're you laughing at?' I asked.

'What a baby you are,' he said and laughed again.

'Don't copy me.'

Then suddenly he swept me up in his arms and lay me down on the bed. *Huh,* I thought, *he probably assumed I'd put up a fight.* I lay there like a doll, my arms and legs limp. When Ali lay down next to me, the bed felt like it was caving in. He tried to touch my breast, but I brushed his hand away. I was embarrassed because it reminded me of how that fat woman, the pimp at the Chinatown brothel I'd been taken to when I first arrived, had examined my body and laughed at my flat chest. But then I realised what Ali wanted. He pulled his shirt off and tried to unbuckle my belt. I put my hands on his chest and pushed him back, and then I undid my own belt and slid out of my trousers. He did the same. When he took off my underwear, I lay still. I was naked. His chest, arms, and legs — nearly his entire body — were covered with dark hair. I wondered, stupidly: *Does eating all that lamb make people grow wool?*

When he pushed inside of me, it hurt so much that my hair stood on end and my spirit nearly left my body. For a moment I saw a woman with her hair covered by a white *hijab*, two little girls, and an old man with a beard and a long tunic standing in a row next to the bed.

That weekend, Ali and I went to see Grandfather Abdul. We were going because I wanted to; Ali was very taken aback at first by the suggestion, but when he heard why, he pursed his lips and thought for a long time with his head down. Then he nodded and agreed. I explained: 'You and I are different from Westerners. I don't know your customs, but where I come from, women don't just sleep with a man they aren't planning to marry. I've decided that I'm going to be your wife.'

I learned something awful later. In his family's home country, daughters and sisters like me who gave their virginity away without their parents' permission could be beaten to death by their fathers and older brothers, and no one would say a thing about it. When we walked into Grandfather Abdul's flat together looking nervous, he frowned but didn't ask us what was wrong. I realised belatedly that he was waiting for us to say something first, so I reached back and pinched Ali on the butt. He let out a small yelp, shot me a look, and then quickly explained why we were there.

'Um, I, uh, want to marry Bari.'

I wanted to yell: *You idiot! You can't just blurt it out like that!* But instead I looked at him and scowled.

'Do you feel the same way, Bari?'

I couldn't bring myself to answer the question out loud, so I just nodded, my head hanging down. Grandfather Abdul looked at us from over his reading glasses.

'Bari, come sit down. Ali, give us some space.'

'Where do you want me to go?'

'Boy, what do I care? Just go down to the pub and get a beer or something! It doesn't matter. But be back in an hour!'

Ali jumped up and hurried out the door. Grandfather Abdul and I were alone. I perched on the edge of a chair across from where he sat.

'How old are you?' he asked.

'I'm eighteen this year.'

'That's young. But then again, when I was your age, people got married even younger than that. However, we are also Muslims who believe in God. Muslims are supposed to marry other Muslims, even though not everyone sticks to that these days. Do you really like Ali?'

I couldn't stop myself from laughing at the question.

'Ali is so silly,' I said. 'He's a big kid.'

'So you do like him. If you two want to marry, I won't stop you. I just want that boy to get his act together, work hard, earn money, and live a good Muslim life. We're in a foreign land. What more can I ask of him?'

Grandfather Abdul asked where we planned to live, and I told him without hesitation that I wanted to get rid of Ali's flat in Shepherd's Bush, where he lived alone, and move in with Grandfather Abdul right away. He had two bedrooms and a living room, and it was already fully furnished. But most of all, I would feel more secure if the three of us lived together.

'I imagine Ali will object,' he said. 'Hang on. The flat across from yours must be vacant now. Why not live there?' He explained that he'd gotten a phone call from the Nigerian woman: her husband had been deported, so she was moving away.

'I don't think we need to preserve all our traditional marriage customs. We can combine the *mayoun* and *mehndi* and hold them here, as a preliminary wedding ceremony that your friends and Ali's can attend; and then the actual wedding can be held at Ali's parents' house in Leeds for neighbours and relatives.'

He brought up their ancestors again.

'My father was a shepherd, but he owned some farmland too. For generations they lived in a village in Kargil, in the northern Indian state of Jammu and Kashmir. He was a follower of Sheikh Abdullah, but after the *sheikh* was arrested, my father took the family and moved to Srinagar.'

Even after I became a part of their family and had lived with them for years, I still hadn't come to understand half of Islamic doctrine, and understood even less of the stories about their ancestors and their home country. When I was growing up, I'd been told that North and South Korea lived differently and thought differently, and therefore had always fought like cats and dogs, and the grown-ups said it was the fault of those big-nosed Americans. The elders in Ali's family likewise told me that Hindus and Muslims had split into India and Pakistan and fought for a long time, that in Indian-occupied Jammu and Kashmir, innocent people were still being rounded up and killed, and that the British were originally to blame for this.

Grandfather Abdul told me innocent civilians were still being killed in this fake war. He said that, when he was young, soldiers would brazenly break down people's doors in broad daylight, storm their houses, and shoot them.

'What's a "fake war"?'

'That's when soldiers murder Muslims in order to steal and do whatever they want, and then report it to their superior officers as "shooting resisters". For that they're rewarded with money and promotions. There was another story like that in the news just recently.'

Grandfather Abdul had returned from the fields one day to find that his wife and two daughters had been shot to death. Ali's father, who was five at the time, was hiding under a water barrel.

'We're the only two in our family who survived.'

Grandfather Abdul and Ali's father fled to London in the mid-1960s, during the height of the conflict in Kashmir.

'I was thirty at the time, and had already lived through everything you can imagine. I got remarried. Men have to get married if they want to save money. When you live alone, you get reckless. A couple of years ago my second wife passed away, and now my only wish left is to make a pilgrimage to Mecca.'

Just then, I remembered the shadowy figures I'd seen in Ali's flat a few days earlier.

'I saw some people in a dream,' I told Grandfather Abdul. 'A lady in a white *hijab* and two girls. Also an elderly man in a tunic and a long beard.'

Grandfather Abdul slowly nodded.

'That was probably Ali's grandmother and our two daughters. The man with the long beard is definitely my father.' His eyes were already filling with tears. He wiped them away with his sleeve. 'Thank you for telling me. If they visited you, then it means they've accepted you as family.'

Ali said he had to talk to his parents before we got

married, and Grandfather Abdul agreed. We decided not to drag it out and made plans to go to Leeds the following Monday, when we were both free. Leeds was north of London, in Yorkshire, two and a half hours away by train. It was a little too far for a day-trip, so we planned on spending the night at Ali's parents' house and returning the next day. Grandfather Abdul called Ali's father first to tell him what was happening, while Ali called his mother. If Ali had told them on his own, they probably would have dismissed it as nonsense.

Ali's house was on the outskirts of Leeds, in a Muslim enclave. Most of the houses in the neighbourhood were painted white and had slab roofs, which made the buildings all look alike. Instead of going out to a yard, neighbours went up to their roofs to drink and talk and have barbecues. Most of the people there were Pakistani. Ali's three younger siblings were still living with their parents. Ali was the second-oldest. His older brother had already married and moved out, while his next-youngest sister lived in the neighbouring city of Bradford with her husband. His mother told us that they would probably only come to the wedding ceremony itself or to the *baraat*, the groom's procession to the wedding.

Ali and I ate lunch in London before taking an afternoon train. He said no one would be home until dinnertime anyway. When we arrived, his mother was waiting for us. She wore a *hijab* with a loose tunic covering her ample figure. She was warm and serene; as I stepped through the door, she gave me a big hug. I mumbled the greeting that Ali had taught me — *as-salamu alaikum* — and she looked me in the eye and said it back. I followed her into the kitchen to try to help her prepare dinner, but she was so adamant that I go sit in the living room with Ali that I turned back. Their home was filled with the distinctive scent of coriander.

Ali's younger sisters returned from school. They giggled the entire time as Ali introduced me, and we shook hands. His younger brother Usman, who worked, didn't return home until it was growing dark. He shook Ali's hand and then shook mine; his grip was so strong that my hand throbbed for a while afterward. Finally, Ali's father came home. His closely cropped hair was speckled with grey, and he had a nice moustache. I could tell at a glance that Ali would look like him when he grew older. Ali's father went into the bedroom and changed into a comfortable traditional outfit. I sat next to Ali without saying a word while his entire family crowded around us and stared at me. Each time his sisters met my eye, they giggled. Ali's father had a kind face, and he didn't say much. When we were seated around the dinner table, his father prayed briefly in their language. When his mother brought out the food, I got up to help her. Everyone seemed warm and loving.

'Where do your parents live?' Ali's father asked.

When I hesitated, Ali answered for me: 'Her parents have both passed away.'

'Oh no,' his mother said. 'I'm so sorry!'

His father said: 'God takes the good ones first,' and then quickly changed the subject.

Ali told them that I'd dreamed about his great-grandfather, his grandmother, and two aunts who died in Srinagar. His father kept eating and didn't say a word, but his mother gently admonished Ali.

'Let's save that story for later.'

When dessert came out, his sisters each grabbed a biscuit and ran off to sit in front of the TV, and his mother went back into the kitchen, leaving the rest of us alone at the table with his father.

Ali's father sipped his *chai* and said, 'Your grandfather told us you two plan to marry. While we're on the subject, I don't think it's a bad idea to rush it a little. You don't want to hold the wedding too close to Ramadan.'

'Yes, Father. That's why we want to get married next month.'

'Next month?' his mother exclaimed. She came running out of the kitchen when she heard that. 'That's *too* fast. You should give yourselves at least half a year to date and get to know each other.'

Ali's father laughed.

'I've already discussed it with your grandfather,' he said. 'We're thinking of buying you a car as a wedding gift. You'll make better money through your minicab business that way, don't you think?'

'Really? Then I won't have to borrow someone else's car and work by the hour.'

'You won't owe me anything, but you will have to repay your grandfather. Yes, now you'll be able to start a new life, raising kids of your own and attending mosque regularly for a change.'

A couple of days after we returned from Leeds, Luna and I were heading home from work after a day at Tongking. A bright light was shining out of the window next door. Curious to know who it was, I knocked on the door. The

Nigerian woman answered it, dressed in an apron and a headscarf. She looked like she'd been packing, and waved me inside. Her belongings were all bundled up.

'I'm moving out tomorrow,' she said. 'The furniture was here when I moved in, but the bed is new. Abdul paid for half of it, so that worked out well for me. He says you're moving in?'

I told her I was, and she clasped my hand.

'Congratulations! Abdul told me you're marrying his grandson.'

She told me what happened to her husband before I had a chance to ask.

'He's definitely being deported. But I can't bear to go back with him. He and I are children of the Biafran civil war.'

I didn't understand.

'Countless children died in that war. What I mean is that he and I survived by the skin of our teeth. He'll do whatever he has to do to make it back.'

Later, Ali explained to me how African refugees would cross the Strait of Gibraltar, travel overland through Europe, and then cross the Strait of Dover into England. The journey to Morocco and across the strait in a tiny boat was incomparably more dangerous than my crossing of the Tumen River. After that, they still had to travel over rugged mountains on foot or stow away on trains, and make it over several national borders before finding a way to get across yet another strait. Refugees trying to make it to London couldn't do it without a lifeline of some kind, at least one person here who could help them get settled.

A minicab driver from Ghana that Ali knew had frittered away three years of his life trying to cross the Strait of Gibraltar. He was caught twice while trying to cross the Strait of Dover from Calais, and finally made it into England by clinging to the roof of the Eurostar. On the approach to the Channel Tunnel, the high-speed train passed through a pair of steep embankments that were built for forty or fifty kilometres on either side of the tracks to protect crops in the surrounding fields. The train had to slow down as it got closer to the tunnel, so refuge-seekers waiting at the top of the embankment would jump onto the roof of the train as it passed. They would cling there for the twenty-minute ride, enduring the high speed and brutal wind. If they made it to the other side, they had to jump off the train before it started to pick up speed again. Railway workers on both the French and British sides sometimes collected the bodies of stowaways who had fallen to their deaths inside the tunnel.

Ali's friend had been inspired to attempt the crossing by a friend's uncle, who was famous back home for making it across that way. But when he got to London and asked around, he learned that his friend's uncle had been dead for years. The man's name alone had served as a symbol of hope, and had kept him going on his journey. We stopped telling our stories in detail, but whenever the subject of our home countries came up, it always seemed to end in fighting and starvation and disease and brutal, fearful generals seizing power. There were still so many people dying in every corner of the world, and people crossing endless borders in search of food, just so they could live without the constant threat of death.

After the Nigerian woman moved out, Ali and I found a little time each evening to work on repainting the walls, fixing the sink, and scrubbing the flat clean from top to bottom. As the layout was the same as the flat I'd shared with Luna, I felt right at home.

The whole process of getting married was called *shadi*, but if I remember correctly, *mayoun* and *mehndi* were the names for the parts of the ceremony where the friends of the bride and groom were invited to eat and exchange gifts the day before the wedding. We held the *mayoun* and *mehndi* in our new flat, but the *baraat* and *valima*, in which we were actually wed, took place at Ali's parents' home in Leeds.

I had no close friends, let alone any of my own flesh and blood in this city, so it was an opportunity to confirm the few, precious relationships I did have with those who had helped me along the way. As Uncle Lou and Uncle Tan were as good as legal guardians to me, I asked if one of them would be willing to be my chaperone. They both said yes and argued over which of them should get to do it, but in the end I assigned the task to Uncle Tan. Though Luna was born in Britain, she was also Bangladeshi, and knew the traditions more or less; she agreed to be my bridesmaid.

Luna and I went to a Muslim butcher shop in the marketplace. The meat was *halal*, which meant that the lamb and chicken had been drained of their blood and blessed. We also bought fish. Ali went to a Pakistani restaurant and ordered all kinds of foods: *chapattis, chaanp, haleem,* fried dumplings, *barfi,* and so on. But I wanted to make a few dishes myself to serve to our wedding guests. Luna and I made lamb and vegetable *tikka* kebabs and a spicy chicken curry with lots of green chillies.

Ali invited his co-workers from the minicab company. Nearly half were Pakistani, while the rest were young Muslims from around Shepherd's Bush. Grandfather Abdul invited a few of his friends from the neighbouring mosque. Ali's two younger sisters skipped school and came down to London to help me. We placed two tables in the courtyard and set them with food and drink and stacks of plates and cups so that the guests could help themselves to as much as they wanted. No one showed up until it started to grow dark. We played a tape of Pakistani music, which had a fast rhythm and a singer with a warbling voice.

Luna told me it wasn't time yet, so we went into her flat and waited. I put on the yellow dress that Grandfather Abdul had bought for me, and wrapped the yellow veil around my head. Luna explained that I had to keep my face covered when I was out there in front of everyone. Then Luna applied a *mehndi* design to my fingers and the backs of my hands using henna paste. She was supposed to draw it on my legs as well, but I told her not to. Vines, leaves, and flowers wound along my skin. Luna was used to giving henna tattoos at the salon; it took her no time at all to recreate the designs. Ali's little sisters opened the door and gestured to us.

'It's time!'

'Hold on!' Luna yelled, a tube of mascara in her hand. 'I need to do her eye makeup.'

She applied black eyeliner and mascara to my eyes. When I glanced in the mirror, the deep-set eyes of a Pakistani woman looked back at me from beneath the yellow veil.

Ali's sisters exclaimed at how pretty I was. I went out to the courtyard and sat in a chair. I had my face covered with the veil, but the light was so bright that I could see everything clearly. The sisters searched for a song, then turned up the volume and sang along. Ali appeared, wearing a white tunic. Luna and his sisters ran to him and sprinkled red rose petals at his feet. When he entered the courtyard, they held a shawl above his head to symbolically shield him from the sky. Ali walked up to a stool set in the middle of the courtyard, and seated himself on it. The guests each came up to him, took out some cash, circled it over his head and gave it to him. His sisters, who were standing next to him, collected the money. Grandfather Abdul and his friends from the mosque danced to the music with their arms raised, while the younger Pakistanis, including Ali's sisters (as well as Luna), danced around in circles.

'The groom is as handsome as a peacock, and the bride is prettier than a flower. God, receive and bless these two.'

Everyone sang, danced, and placed sweets in my mouth. When I turned my head to try to refuse more, they stuffed them in anyway. As it was an informal ceremony, there was only one round of singing and dancing, and then everyone gathered around the tables to eat. Everyone kept calling for me to join them, so Ali lifted my veil and I rewrapped it around my hair as a *hijab*.

As the non-Muslim guests would have been disappointed if there was no alcohol, beer had been provided as well. Uncle Tan gave a short speech, and then Uncle Lou stood up and started to give a toast — but he suddenly choked up and had to turn around to wipe his tears. I knew without his having to say anything that he was thinking of the daughter he'd left behind.

The actual wedding ceremony was being held the very next day in Leeds, so we left early the next morning in a van borrowed from Ali's workplace, accompanied by Uncle Tan, Luna, Ali's sisters, and Grandfather Abdul.

When we arrived, the front yard was already crowded with people. Ali's siblings were there along with his parents, relatives, friends, neighbours, and people from the mosque. There were close to a hundred guests altogether. Ali's parents had obtained permission from their neighbours to put up an awning in their yard in order to accommodate the overflow of guests, and seats were prepared for friends and relatives up on the roof.

I went up first and sat down to wait for my groom. Ali was downstairs in the yard, greeting all the guests. His sisters and friends placed flower garlands around the necks of Ali's parents and Grandfather Abdul. They placed another one around Ali's neck as he was coming up the stairs. When he was finally next to me, we greeted the guests, who gave me gifts of money. We signed the marriage contract, which was officiated by an *imam*. Luna and a friend of Ali's sister who lived in Bradford served as my witnesses. Two of Ali's friends who'd gone to school with him in Leeds were his witnesses. Then we took dozens of photos, went downstairs to greet the guests from the neighbourhood as bride and groom, and were given more wedding gifts of cash. We spent the next day resting in the comfort of close family. Then Grandfather Abdul, Luna, Ali, and I returned to London. I was in a daze for the next few days from all that sensory overload.

Ali used the money that his father and grandfather had given him to purchase a used Volkswagen estate car that wasn't too old. He signed a contract with the minicab company as an official driver and car owner. Now he only had to pay call fees to the company, but was his own boss otherwise.

Uncle Lou and Uncle Tan had spent a lot of money on our wedding. Uncle Tan not only gave us three hundred pounds as a wedding gift, he'd also given me a thousand-pound advance on my wages. Uncle Lou had gifted us two hundred pounds.

But he gave me an even bigger gift besides that.

A few days after the wedding, he came to the store and told me that my smuggling debt was nearly paid in full, and as I was now married to a British citizen, wouldn't I like to apply for a real passport and obtain a residence visa? The passport I'd been given when I was smuggled into the country had been bought by the snakeheads from a forger, and would be detected immediately by immigration officials. Uncle Lou said he could get me the passport of a recently deceased Chinese woman who'd had a legal residency visa. He'd joked with me once that no matter how many people in Europe's Chinatowns get sick and die or pass away of old age, the populations never get any smaller. When I thought about being able to register my marriage officially and receive a work permit, I decided it didn't matter how much it would take to purchase the dead woman's passport. It would probably cost me at least five thousand pounds, but Ali and I could find a way to earn money and pay down the debt.

I thought about the deal Princess Bari made with the

totem pole in my grandmother's stories: *three by three is nine* — nine years spent giving him a son and caring for his home in exchange for passage, firewood, and water.

I realised that life means waiting, enduring the passage of time. Nothing ever quite meets our expectations, yet as long as we are alive, time flows on, and everything eventually comes to pass.

TEN

Ali and I moved into the flat the Nigerian couple had lived in, but we decided to use his grandfather's kitchen upstairs to cook. That way, the three of us could eat together as a family. As soon as I got home from work in the evenings, I cooked dinner using whatever Grandfather Abdul had picked up at the market that afternoon based on the note that we'd left for him, but it was often just Grandfather Abdul and me. As the weekends kept Ali busy, he usually took a couple of days in the middle of the week to rest during the day and work the late shift after dinner.

With so much time for just the two of us, Grandfather Abdul and I talked much more often than we used to. He told me all about his family and his ancestors, about the One and Only God, Allah, and stories of the Prophet Muhammad. I couldn't read the Qur'an, but I ended up memorising the first verse of the Islamic creed: *'La ilaha illallah, Muhammad rasulullah'* ('There is no god but God, Muhammad is the Messenger of God'). But this wasn't surprising to me: ever since I was little, Grandmother used to say there was a Lord in Heaven who presided over all of Creation. Whenever my father caught her talking that way, he would browbeat her and say it was just superstition. To me, there wasn't much difference between the being my grandmother had talked about and the being Grandfather Abdul described. I guess you could say it was like the difference between them eating *naan* and *chapatti*, and us eating rice.

Sometimes I talked about my grandmother. Grandfather Abdul said that because she was a good person, she would now be an angel in a Paradise filled with flowing rivers and flowers in full bloom. I pictured her mingling with the other good people somewhere in a field of flowers beyond the rainbow bridge that I saw in my visions.

I also told him about the other people in my life: Uncle Tan was a Buddhist, and Uncle Lou used his breaks from filling orders in the kitchen to recite endless prayers that sounded like magic spells. Many of the people who lived in Chinatown went to a Taoist temple to burn incense and pray. Luna was Bangladeshi and Auntie Sarah Sri Lankan, but as they were both born in Britain, they went to church and believed in Jesus. Nevertheless, they each skilfully balanced the etiquette and rules of their religion with their own cultural heritage. Grandfather Abdul smiled with satisfaction at my descriptions of everyone.

'Child, just as our clothes and food are a little different from each other's, our lifestyles are also different. But that's all. Providence converges into one.'

Though I knew nearly nothing about Islam, Ali's family's customs were not all that difficult for me. Later, Ramadan was a little tough to get through, but once the period of fasting was over, I realised anew the preciousness of family and daily meals. When I told Grandfather Abdul the story of Princess Bari and how I got my name, he smiled brightly and nodded.

'If your destiny is the same as the Bari of legend, then I guess it's time for you to start looking for the life-giving water.'

'I don't know, Grandfather. All my grandmother told me was that the water would find *me*.'

The days passed, tranquil and untroubled. Ali worked hard at his taxi job, and I continued giving foot massages at the salon. Five times a day, Grandfather Abdul spread out his prayer rug and bowed in the direction of Mecca, and on Fridays Ali joined him at the mosque. In the privacy of our flat, I learned how to pray by copying Ali.

One day, I was working at Tongking when my afternoon client arrived.

'America is at war!' she exclaimed the moment she came in. 'I just saw it on TV. The whole world is going mad!'

There were shocked whispers all over the salon. Uncle Tan brought the television out of the break room and plugged it in. Sure enough, every single channel was broadcasting the news about what had happened in New York. They kept showing the same footage over and over, of a passenger plane flying into a building and exploding, and then another plane following suit. We held our breaths at first, as if we were watching an action movie. But when the building collapsed all at once, we screamed. People running down streets covered in broken glass and dust and smoke; the horrified faces and torn clothes of the wounded, who had barely made it out alive; paper and debris blowing around in the wind.

By the time I got home that night, it seemed the whole world had lost its mind over the events in New York. I went upstairs to find Grandfather Abdul kneeling on his rug, about to pray. I waited just outside the door for him to finish. He stood, bowed once more and turned around.

'You saw the news?' he asked. My face fell. I nodded.

'I called Ali,' he said. 'I told him to come home early tonight.'

I understood what he was implying. Grandfather Abdul kept peering out the window until Ali was back. He did return much earlier than usual, but Grandfather Abdul still looked angry when he came in.

'What took you so long? I told you to come home early.'

'Someone called asking me to take them to the airport. I was on my way back.'

'Stay home in the evening from now on. If you have to work late, only do it on the weekend.'

Ali glanced at me and then spread his arms wide and asked: 'What are you so worried about?'

'The world is different now! Even before this happened, Muslims were not looked at kindly.'

'Grandfather, that's America. We're British.'

'Legally, yes. But now they'll be more open about criticising our religion, and our way of life.'

Ali looked frustrated. 'The terrorists are extremists!' he shouted. 'They have nothing to do with Muslims like us!'

Grandfather Abdul sighed. 'But they're still Muslim. Terrible things are going to happen. This has given them an excuse.'

I prepared dinner quietly and didn't interrupt them. We ate in silence.

Grandfather Abdul's predictions weren't far off: a rock was thrown through the window of the mosque; women wearing *hijabs* were cursed at; and graffiti was spray-painted on the homes of Muslims.

More than two months later, it was Ramadan. Ali would awaken at dawn to eat a little soup or rice porridge, then touch nothing else until nightfall except the occasional sip of water. I didn't feel right enjoying my lunch with the other studio employees, so I just had juice or something else to drink. As my shift didn't end until after dark, I could go ahead and eat as soon as I got home; but I ate more lightly than usual, and avoided anything too fatty. Mostly it was porridge, vegetables, or fruit. By that point, I was halfway to living a Muslim lifestyle and observing the customs.

One night, Ali received a phone call. From his voice, I figured it was his father. When he hung up, he looked grim.

'What's wrong?'

'Usman has disappeared.'

'Doesn't he work at a factory?'

'He does. But he said he was taking time off to travel with friends.'

'Then what's the problem?'

Ali shook his head.

'They found the receipt for the plane ticket in his room. That idiot has gone to Pakistan.'

There was a knock at the door. Grandfather Abdul stepped inside.

'Your father just called. I take it you spoke to him, too,

about Usman going to Pakistan?'

They both fell silent. Grandfather Abdul looked deep in thought.

'You better go to Leeds yourself to try to find out what happened,' he said to Ali. 'Young people mistake friendship for not telling their elders what their friends are doing. Your brother's friends aren't going to tell your parents the truth.'

Ali nodded and said: 'I know Usman's friends. They'll know what's going on.'

I interrupted them: 'I don't understand what all the fuss is about. So your brother went back home? I'm sure he'll be back in a few days, smiling about the nice vacation he had.'

Grandfather Abdul shook his head slowly from side to side.

'It's not like that. The United States and Britain have declared war on Afghanistan, which means that calls for support and solidarity have been going out to young Muslim men in other countries.'

Ali left for Leeds the next day. Grandfather Abdul and I waited and didn't eat until he returned, late that night. His long arms looked like they were sagging all the way to his knees, no doubt from worry and fatigue. As soon as Ali collapsed onto Grandfather Abdul's soft couch, Grandfather Abdul started pressing him for information.

'What did you find out?'

'He's in Pakistan. He's already been there for over three weeks. He went with four guys from his youth group.'

'Did you find out where exactly he went?'

'Peshawar. One of the guys, Saeed, is from there.'

'Did you get Saeed's address?'

'Yes, from Saeed's mother. She asked me to go find him and bring him back.'

It was all but certain that they were headed for Afghanistan, as Peshawar was right on the border, a few hours from Kabul.

Now that Ali knew his younger brother's whereabouts, there was nothing I could do to stop him; his purpose in going there was to prevent something terrible from happening to his family. I had not yet told Ali, but I was almost three months pregnant at the time. Everyone was anxious to find Usman, so Ali left for Pakistan just a couple of days later. None of us knew it would be a long farewell.

By the following summer, Ali still had not returned; nor had there been any word from him. I gave birth without him, to a baby girl with dark skin and big eyes just like her father's. I had just turned nineteen.

A new government had been installed in Afghanistan since the beginning of the year, but the news continued to broadcast reports stating that military operations to root out insurgents in the mountains were ongoing. Every day, the television showed refugee camps, torn-up streets, and starving children.

I spent two days in the hospital. Grandfather Abdul took Ali's place and ran around buying baby clothes, baby bottles, diapers, and other supplies. He named the baby 'Hurriyah'.

'What does *hurriyah* mean?' I asked him.

'It means *freedom.*'

I murmured the Korean word for freedom under my breath: *jayu*. Words need objects to attach to if they're to be remembered. I thought about the names of the wildflowers

203

that used to brighten the hills at the foot of Mount Baekdu as well as the banks of the Tumen River, where a bleak wind used to blow: purple, yellow, and white *nancho*; childlike *dongja*; starry-eyed *wangbyeol*; delicate *jebi*, named after a bird; *eunbangul*, which resembled little silver bells; *jaunyeong*, the tips of their petals dipped in magenta; bristly *jilgyeongi*, on thick green stems; china-pink *paeraengi*; dark purple *norugwi*; *babpul*, which looked like they held little grains of rice; and the cute yellow buttercups we called *minari ajaebi*. The list was endless. I pictured myself running through fields of them with my sisters, and looked down at the baby asleep next to me with her eyes gently closed. To the name Hurriyah, I added the Korean name that signified *girl*: Suni. I murmured under my breath again: *Hurriyah Suni*.

Luna dropped by after work each night to fix me some food and help look after the baby. Ali's parents also came to visit once, with Ali's younger sisters. At the same time that they were thrilled the baby looked so much like her father, they couldn't hide their tears. Before they left, Ali's father hugged me and whispered in my ear:

'Ali's older brother is going to Pakistan to look for him this summer. He'll send us good news.'

I just smiled and didn't say anything; I knew Ali was still alive.

I didn't go back to work at the salon until the baby was over a hundred days old, but I continued going to Lady Emily's once a week. Most of the time, she only wanted a massage, but some days she would tell me about her dreams instead, or confide in me about her communication with her deceased nanny, Becky. She had several psychic friends, and they all took turns meeting at each other's houses. Lady Emily had offered to introduce me to the group, but I always found an excuse to decline. One day, I arrived at Lady Emily's house in Holland Park at our scheduled time, only to find Auntie Sarah looking grim.

'Madam is out. She's gone to Brighton,' she said.

'Did something bad happen?' I asked.

Auntie Sarah lowered her voice: 'Her husband's dead. Shot.'

'What? How …?'

'That little bitch shot him three times.'

Auntie Sarah stopped there and wouldn't elaborate. I was so shocked that I forgot all about my own worries, and felt bad for Lady Emily. I'd figured her preoccupation with psychics was because of her separation from her husband.

Luna, the baby, and I were spending the evening together that night when Grandfather Abdul came downstairs. He stroked Hurriyah Suni's tiny feet and rubbed his beard against her soft-as-water cheek.

'I need to tell you something,' he began.

'I'll give you two some privacy,' Luna said. She got up and started to head for the door, but Grandfather Abdul gestured for her to stay.

'It's okay,' he said. 'You two tell each other everything anyway. Ali's older brother just got back from Pakistan.'

Luna and I exchanged a glance, and both looked expectantly at Grandfather Abdul.

'He confirmed that Ali went from Peshawar to Kabul in search of his brother. Also, Saeed's uncle, who lives in

Peshawar, said that Usman and his friends stayed with him for five days before leaving for Kabul. We know this much because Ali made one phone call from Kabul. But like his younger brother, he hasn't been heard from since. According to reports, Jalalabad, which is near Kabul, and northern Kunduz were bombed by the Northern Alliance, and a lot of people died or were taken away. I can only hope that they're still safe somehow.'

I thought to myself: *Ali is alive. I can feel it.*

It had been months since Ali had left for Afghanistan, with no contact and no trace of his whereabouts, so it was only natural that almost everyone assumed he and his brother were dead. Luna and Grandfather Abdul kept their heads down and wouldn't look at me or say anything. Lately, everyone had been doing the same whenever Ali came up in conversation. They thought it was too late to try to comfort me by telling me not to worry, that he would be back soon. But I had seen Ali in my dreams. I'd seen Usman as well. Maybe because Ali was my husband, he was always talking or laughing or getting angry, just as in real life, but Usman would only stand at a distance and watch me, or would turn and walk away even as I called out to him.

One day, Auntie Sarah called while I was working at Tongking. It wasn't Lady Emily's scheduled day, but she asked me to hurry over. I took a cab. As soon as I walked in, Auntie Sarah gestured for me to follow her upstairs.

'What's wrong?' I asked.

She shook her head and sighed.

'She's asked me three times whether you've arrived yet. She's a mess. Do whatever you can.'

When I entered the bedroom, the curtains were drawn and the lights were out. The room was completely dark.

Auntie Sarah called out timidly: 'Madam, Bari is here.'

'Okay.'

Lady Emily's voice was very faint. Auntie Sarah gave me a push and disappeared. I kept going in the direction of the push, and came to a stop at the side of the bed. I couldn't see a thing, so I had to switch on the bedside lamp. A bottle of cognac sat on the nightstand next to a round snifter. Lady Emily was drunk. I crouched down near her pillow.

'Shall I prepare a massage?' I asked.

'That stupid man took three bullets to the back. They told me to ID his body, and then they pulled back the sheet. He'd grown so old in the last few years that I barely recognised him. He had lost so much hair too. And oh, that big belly of his! Hideous.'

I listened quietly. Outside, fat clouds drifted through a clear blue sky, and the leaves on the trees that lined the road were green and beautiful. But Lady Emily lay half-naked, covered only by an untied bathrobe, her limbs splayed. Her sagging breasts were like half-empty leather flasks.

'Turns out that whore had a lover back home in Thailand,' Lady Emily said. 'She flew back three or four times a year to see him. Probably stole a lot of money, too. I bet she got sick of sleeping with an old man and was out of her mind when she shot him. The police asked if I wanted to see her. Why would I want to see that murdering bitch?'

Lady Emily covered her face with her hands and began to sob hysterically. She turned on her side and pulled her knees up to her chest. I tried to console her as I straightened her limbs out, covered her with a towel, and began to massage her shoulders.

'Okay,' I said. 'Forget about the awful thing that happened. Just let it go. The memory will fade in time. Don't let it consume you.'

Her knotted muscles began to soften as I rubbed and kneaded. I made my way down the backs of her thighs to her calves and down to her feet. As I squeezed and stroked her feet, my eyes closed automatically. I shivered and my shoulders trembled; my body seemed to grow colder and lighter much more quickly than usual.

—

Someone is standing in the dark: a figure dressed in a loosely draped, dark brown garment made from a rough fabric. I recognise the apparition as Lady Emily's nanny, Becky.

Please help her, I murmur.

In a hoarse voice, she says: *You're in no position to be worried about others.*

I say that we speak, but in fact we use no words. No sooner do she and I think of the same place than the furniture in the room vanishes and the darkness lifts. We stand in the middle of a parched land rough with rocks and dry grass. Wrinkles crease the corners of Becky's dark eyes as she gazes out over the windswept expanse.

Aren't you looking for your husband? she asks.

Where are we?

The middle place, between the world of the living and the

world of the dead, where shamans like you and I can come and go. Even after death, we can traverse this place.

Am I dead, then?

You die and return to life. There's something here you want to see.

In an instant the sky turns black as night, and a loud noise like thunder booms. Lights flash around us. Machine guns rattle, and the sound of cannons threatens to tear my eardrums. I glide over the rugged land. A small village appears. Black smoke rises, and I see houses on fire. People pour out of a narrow alleyway. Bodies lie in the street. Men with missing arms and legs scream. I hear planes and helicopters overhead. Tanks roll into the village on their metal wheels.

I run like mad until I see a mosque in front of an empty lot, and rush into the corridor. Inside, hundreds of men and women are praying, their bodies prostrate on the stone floor. They keep bowing, standing up and kneeling down in silence, over and over. I ask the women, some in full *burqa* and others with only *hijabs* covering their hair: *Have you seen Ali?*

Ali? Who's Ali?

Anyone here seen Ali?

Their questions fly back and forth through the mosque until the entire place is filled with their voices. I hear someone at the far end call out to me: *I saw Usman. He went to Kunduz.*

Murmurs of *Usman, Usman* and *Kunduz, Kunduz* spread through the mosque again. I push my way through the crowd in search of the speaker of that voice. But they all turn their backs when I get close. I keep pushing, burrowing further into the mosque. Someone grabs me by the scruff of the neck, and I am propelled between the pillars and back out to the corridor.

Those are the spirits of the dead, Becky says. *They're all stopped at their memories from when they were alive.*

Is this Hell?

No, it's like a way station. There's no such thing as Heaven or Hell. If they work hard, they'll be able to move on to a better place, the same way that babies are born and grow up. Souls with many sins take longer and are stuck at a lower spot.

I think of Kunduz, and immediately a dusty street, a bell tower and low houses appear. I see a plaza in the village where a market is held. There are wooden display stands and awning poles. But the streets are empty, and the houses are all shuttered. I hear a sharp whistling sound followed by an explosion. Dust billows up like a cloud and blocks out the sky. A shell lands in the plaza, and a large crater appears. Another shell lands on the roof of a house. Cement and stone shards fall like hail.

I picture the outside of the village, and in a flash I see a group of men standing with their arms in the air on the side of a road overgrown with dry weeds. There are several trucks. Soldiers with bare feet and military jackets over their tunics aim guns at the men. An officer shouts, and the soldiers fire. The men collapse; several break away and run. They fall face-first. The image vanishes, and it grows dark as the ground ripples with their crawling bodies. I run over to them.

Usman! Is there anyone here named Usman?

I hear a familiar voice behind me.

Bari? What are you doing here?

I turn, and Usman is standing there, tall and with big hands just like his older brother. He has a long beard that makes him look ten years older.

Ali came looking for you. Did you see him?

We parted ways immediately.

Shapes, wavering like wisps of smoke, watch as soldiers toss their bodies into trucks.

In a flash I am whisked away on the wind to where the land ends. I see sand and open water. Towering behind me are enormous mountains carrying heavy loads of snow on their heads. Becky stands next to me and gazes out over the ocean.

Your husband is at sea, she says.

Where is he going?

I don't know, but it looks as if he's headed to where the sun sets in the world of the living.

Help me. Please take me there.

When I plead with her, Becky gives me the same cold, expressionless look that she had when I first saw her in front of the bonfire.

Everyone suffers, she says. *But they have to fix their own problems. That's true for Emily and true for you, too. Now let me ask you this: why can't I be with him?*

Who?

My husband in the world beyond.

Let's go look for him.

I can't find him. He left long ago, on a ship. I spent my wedding night with a wooden effigy. The village elders all

211

remember his name. They say he was a brave warrior who hunted lions.

We gaze out at an endless sea that is so blue it is nearly black.

—

I opened my eyes slowly, very slowly, as if peeling off strips of wet paper that had been gluing my eyelids shut. The world around me changed, and I was back in my body. Lady Emily was still asleep. I got up and pulled back the curtain: it was already after dark. I thought again about the scenes of war and Usman's death that I had seen so clearly. I remembered how Ali had not appeared even once, and I pictured the beach to which Becky had taken me. I was certain that Ali was still alive somewhere. When I was a child in North Korea, the adults taught me that if I truly wanted something with all of my heart, then I shouldn't tell anyone or it would never happen, it would only slip further out of my reach. I made up my mind that I would not tell anyone how certain I was that Usman was dead and Ali alive. I decided to hide it from Grandfather Abdul as well.

ELEVEN

Xiang came to Tongking several days after the Lunar New Year, looking for me. I was with a client. Vinh, who'd finished with her client first and was resting outside in the waiting room, poked her head through the doorway and waited for me to look up. I looked at her questioningly, and she gestured behind her with her thumb. I assumed she meant someone was waiting to see me.

I wrapped a hot towel around the client's feet and went out into the waiting room. I didn't recognise the woman there at first. She wore a short skirt, boots that came all the way up to her knees, and a loose jumper that left her shoulders bare. Her hair was long, straight, and parted down the middle like a stereotype of an East Asian girl. She sat with her legs crossed, but stood up halfway when she saw me, raising her butt off the chair awkwardly.

'How've you been?' she asked.

I could not for the life of me place her smile.

'I'm sorry ... Do I know you?'

I tilted my head to one side as I looked at her, and she answered in a small voice: 'I'm Xiang.'

For a moment I thought: *Who's Xiang?* Then I clapped my hand over my mouth. She looked so much older that she was almost unrecognisable. Her once-pale face had turned dark, and the once-taut skin around her eyes was sagging, but what made it even harder to tell that it was Xiang was her caked-on makeup. I clasped her hand in surprise. At that instant, a rush of regret, like a kind of guilt, came over me.

'I meant to look for you,' I said. 'But other things kept getting in the way. I'm so sorry …'

'I only need a minute of your time. Are you busy?'

'No, I have time.'

I took her across the street to a café. When she rested her hands on the table, I saw that her nail polish was chipped, and that the seams in her jumper were coming undone. She kept glancing at the counter and then at the entrance, as if she was nervous about something.

'Lou told me where to find you,' she said.

'Have you been in that same place this whole time?'

'I moved around a bit … Situation's the same.'

What she meant by 'the same', of course, was that she was still working in brothels. As she and I had been through so much together, there was no need to beat around the bush.

'Have you considered finding a different line of work?' I asked.

'What's it matter now?' Xiang said. 'Anyway, I'm doing fine.' But then she pressed both hands against the table suddenly, leaned forward, and blurted out the words she'd been trying to keep inside: 'Loan me some money! I'm really in a jam, and you're the only one I could think of.'

I didn't want to tell her that I'd already paid off my smuggling debt, or ask how much she still owed. The only reason I'd managed to free myself was because Uncle Lou had been willing to vouch for me, but for all I knew she might still have been in the snakeheads' clutches.

'How much do you need?' I asked.

'Two hundred pounds. Or even just a hundred.'

'I don't have any cash on me, but I'll get it for you.'

Xiang waited in the café while I went back to the salon and asked Uncle Tan for a hundred-pound advance on my wages. She gulped down two glasses of water in quick succession. When I handed her the five twenty-pound notes, she grabbed the cash and got up immediately.

'Look at the time,' she said. 'I swear I'll pay you back next week.'

She went outside, waved goodbye, and then ran in the direction of the Underground. I stood on the sidewalk and stared after her. She never once looked back.

Something wasn't sitting right with me, so when my shift at the salon ended I called Uncle Lou. He didn't have long to talk, because they were getting ready for the dinner rush. When I told him that Xiang had come to see me and asked how she'd been living, he apologised right away.

'She begged and pleaded, saying she wanted to see you, so I had no choice but to give her the address. That girl isn't going to make it. I'm pretty sure she's on drugs. She can't go back to China either. It's really sad. Anyway, I'll pay back what she borrowed from you.'

I told him it didn't matter and asked whether or not there was anything he could do for her.

He sighed. 'You have to have the will to live first. That's the only way you can earn other people's trust and get help.'

Naturally, Xiang did not come back the following week. I had no intention of collecting on the debt, but decided to use my next day off to try to track her down. I thought that if we opened up to each other, we could find some way to help her. That was my plan, but somehow I never found the time to follow through.

One night, I happened to miss the last Underground train while coming home from a friend's birthday party with Luna. We boarded a night bus near Piccadilly Circus instead. Sitting in the back of the bus was a large group of drunken girls dressed in short skirts and wearing bright makeup and garish accessories. They chattered loudly; one was slumped in her seat, asleep. As I looked at them, I noticed an East Asian woman behind them gazing vacantly at the passing streetlights. She must have felt me staring at her, because she turned and looked at me. Our eyes locked. The expression on her face was so dark that I couldn't look away. When she got off the bus on some quiet street, I kept looking intently out the window at her. She stood and stared back at me. I felt as if I was looking at Xiang. *Ah,* I thought, *the ties that bind us were already formed long ago, in the heavens. Like a finely woven spider web that ensnares us all.*

Ali had still not come home, and there was still no news; meanwhile, Hurriyah Suni had grown rapidly and was crawling everywhere, grabbing onto things to try to stand up, falling down and crying. I would leave her upstairs with Grandfather Abdul while I went to work, but it wasn't easy for him to keep up with her. Some days I came home to

216

find him and his great-granddaughter conked out together on the bed. He finally asked his friends at the mosque for help finding a babysitter, and ended up hiring the daughter of a Pakistani family that ran a small corner shop selling cigarettes, bus tickets, accessories, and other such items. The son went to school, while the daughter, Ayesha, helped out at the shop. Ayesha agreed to look after Hurriyah in the afternoons, when her mother took over for her at the store. Grandfather Abdul offered to pay for the babysitting, but I firmly refused. It was my child after all, and even if he was a blood relative, he was already doing so much just by taking care of her in the mornings.

I hadn't been to Lady Emily's house in nearly a month, as she was travelling frequently around that time. When I finally returned, Auntie Sarah greeted me at the door with a smile. I'd long been in the habit of guessing the mood of the rest of the house by the look on her face when I arrived, so the moment I saw her, I said: 'I take it something good has happened.'

'An angel's come down from Heaven,' she said, practically humming the words.

I gestured to show I didn't understand, and she turned to lead the way.

'Let's hurry upstairs. The madam has some bragging to do.'

We headed for the stairs, but I could already hear the breathless giggling of a child coming from the living room. Lady Emily was clapping her hands and shouting. We stood and watched for a moment as the two of them scampered around the room in a game of tag.

'Ah, Bari!' Lady Emily said when she noticed me. 'Come in and meet Anthony.'

The boy was running toward me, so I scooped him up on reflex. His face crumpled into a startled frown. He reared out of my arms, reaching for Auntie Sarah, who stood next to me, so I passed him over to her. He was a handsome little boy with black hair, dark eyes, and fine features.

'Take him into the kitchen and give him something to eat,' Lady Emily said.

Auntie Sarah took the child downstairs while Lady Emily and I had tea. She told me the baby belonged to her late husband and his Thai mistress. Her husband's sister had been looking after him while the mother was in jail, awaiting trial for the murder. The sister-in-law had called her a while back and, after some hesitation, Lady Emily had gone to see the child herself. The moment she saw him, she knew she had to bring him home.

'My heart felt like it was caving in the first time I saw him.'

She already had one child — a grown daughter who'd married an Australian man — but said the moment she brought the boy home, the house seemed to come back to life, and that she even felt as if she was growing younger.

I looked around at the living room, its curtains open wide for a change. 'The house feels different now,' I said with a nod. 'That's a good sign.'

'You know, it's the strangest thing,' she said. 'The hatred I used to feel toward Anthony's mother is fading. The mere thought of her would fill me with indignation, and I held all Southeast Asian women in low regard.'

As I massaged her feet, I felt her body relax. Her good mood must have transmitted itself to me, because the anxiety and frustration that had been weighing me down for so long seemed to lift as well.

It was early summer, and Hurriyah Suni was a month away from her first birthday. Rain had been falling all day, making it dark inside the salon even though we were nowhere near closing time yet. I turned up the lights. The rainy weather outside seemed even darker and drearier. Uncle Tan suggested closing the salon early, and everyone seemed to agree that the weather called for it.

When Luna and I walked out of the salon, a woman who had been standing under the eaves of the building next door blocked our path. I recognised her immediately this time.

'Xiang!'

Xiang wore an oversized coat that looked like an army field-jacket over her skirt. She must have been standing in the rain for some time, because her wet hair was stuck to her head.

'I've been waiting for you,' she said.

I grabbed her hand involuntarily. 'Come home with us,' I said. 'You'll get sick if you stay out here.'

I pulled her under my umbrella with me. Luna kept glancing over at us as we walked. Xiang asked us to wait a moment in front of a small shop while she ran inside. Luna turned to me as if she'd been waiting for an opportunity.

'Who is she?'

'An old friend from back home.'

'She looks homeless. Is this safe?'

'She's been going through a rough time. I have to help her.'

Xiang had gone in to buy a pack of cigarettes. As soon as she came out, she ripped open the pack, lit one up, and puffed away on it feverishly. When we got to our building, Luna went into her own flat without saying a word, and I knocked on the door to mine. The door swung open and Ayesha greeted me.

'I think Hurriyah can tell when her mum is coming home. She kept whining and refusing to go to bed.'

Hurriyah Suni was sitting on the floor surrounded by wooden blocks, but she crawled over to me quickly when I came in, already on the verge of tears. I picked her up and wished Ayesha a good night.

'What pretty eyes,' Xiang murmured.

'Did you eat dinner? I'll make something for us.'

'I'm fine with *ramen*.'

'Really? That's good. Actually, I was a little worried. It was raining too hard to get groceries.'

While I was heating up a bottle for Hurriyah, I turned to see Xiang putting a cigarette in her mouth.

'If you have to smoke, please go outside to do it,' I warned her.

She looked surprised, then put the cigarette back in the pack and sat on the sofa with her knees drawn up. I fed Hurriyah first and changed her diaper, then gently patted her on the back while singing old lullabies. She soon fell asleep. I put her to bed and came back into the living room to find Xiang sniffling and crying.

'What's wrong?'

'Hearing those lullabies reminded me of when I was young.' She grabbed a tissue to blow her nose and wipe her eyes. 'I'm sorry I haven't paid you back.'

'It's fine. Take your time …'

I asked her questions while we ate.

'Are the snakeheads still bothering you?'

'No. After about a year, they handed me over to a new house and cancelled my debt.'

'Why don't you go to the police? If you get deported as an illegal alien, then at least you'll get to go back home.'

'I don't want to go home. I like it here.'

'Then find a new job. You could do foot massages like me. I'll talk to my boss.'

Xiang chuckled. 'It's too late for that …' She wouldn't look me in the eye. 'Everywhere I go, it's all the same.'

We slept beside each other for the first time in a long time. Before falling asleep, we lay in the dark and talked about everything she'd been through in London. She told me about the girls brought over from Asia, Russia, and Eastern Europe to work in neighbourhoods like this one. About women whose families went through hell to find them and take them back home, only to watch as the women returned within half a year. About accepting money to sleep with just anyone, with people you didn't love, trusting and relying on the man who pimps you out because you believe he's your lover. About the kinds of things that take place in every city in every part of the world.

Right before we fell asleep, Xiang murmured something in the dark: 'No matter how hard I try, I can't seem to remember Zhou's face anymore.'

'Zhou?'

'My husband … We left him behind in Dalian, remember?'

In a voice as sleep-addled as hers, I said: 'That's right. He didn't make it onto the boat.'

We didn't say anything more. I slipped into a deep sleep.

—

I see a barren land devoid of even a single tree. White-hot sunlight blazes down on sand — just the sight of it makes my throat parched and my chest heavy. Inside a square wire fence shaped like a chicken coop, someone kneels in a fetal position with his head pressed to the ground. His hands are tied behind him. I cannot see his face, but I recognise those familiar shoulders right away: there's no doubt it's Ali.

Ali! I shout. *What are you doing?*

No sound. I can't move toward him. He keeps shifting a tiny bit to the right and then to the left, as if he's in pain, before kneeling straight again. I struggle to move, and call his name.

I stand in a dark corridor. On each side, small windows reveal tiny cells in which men are stripped naked and kneeling. I call out for my husband and they each turn to look at me, but their faces are hooded in darkness. Then I hear shouts.

Do not move! Do not speak! Do not get up! What're you looking at? On your knees! You son of a bitch! You piece of shit!

I hear voices moaning and protesting.

So thirsty. It hurts. So hungry. Don't hit me. You assholes.

Mother! Wife! Save me!

I find Ali lying on his side on a dirt floor with his arms wrapped around his knees. I stand in front of the window and shout: 'Honey, it's me! It's Bari! Please get up!'

Now I know he can hear me. He flinches and lifts his head.

I shout again, impatient: 'Here! I'm right here!'

He staggers to his feet and lunges toward the window. 'Bari! Bari!'

I study his face. His head is shaved and his beard has grown long, but his big, skittish eyes are the same. Tears spill down his cheeks. My body is whisked away on a rough breeze and carried back down the corridor into darkness.

~

'Ali!' I scream, and sit up in bed. The window that faces onto the courtyard glows a milky white. A turtle dove sings plaintively outside. Xiang is sleeping on her side. Oh, why did I have to see his face so clearly in my dream? I lay there stunned, unable to go back to sleep.

I lay like that all night, unable to do anything. Only when Hurriyah Suni woke up and started crying because she was hungry did I drag myself out of bed to fix her a bottle and some baby cereal. I couldn't erase the image of Ali's face suddenly appearing in the darkness. I set my daughter down on the floor to play by herself while I prepared breakfast for Xiang and me.

'Xiang, come eat.'

I tried to wake her, but she frowned and struggled to raise her head.

'I don't eat breakfast,' she said, and rolled over and went back to sleep.

I ate breakfast alone and then asked Luna to tell our boss that I couldn't go to work that day. I told her I wasn't feeling well.

When the minutes clicked by and I didn't show up upstairs, Grandfather Abdul came down.

'I decided to stay home today,' I told him. I debated whether to tell him about my dream, but decided to hold off.

'Okay,' he said. 'Looks like you have a visitor?'

'Yes, an old friend from back home.'

'Then I guess I'd better use this opportunity to go out for a change.'

He would probably drop by the mosque or to one of the neighbourhood parks to have a leisurely chat with his friends. I played with Hurriyah and then heated up some food for Xiang, who didn't wake up until noon. Ayesha showed up in the afternoon, but when she saw I was there she headed back home. For the first time that day, I discovered how dirty the house was: all the blankets and rugs were soiled with spilled food and the baby's spit-up. I pulled the sheets off of the mattress, undid the duvet covers, and packed up the bedding with Hurriyah's dirty clothes and my own. I looked down at her as she scampered from this toy to that, first chasing after a rabbit that hopped at the push of a button, then playing with a doll that could speak.

'Xiang, would you mind if I ran over to the laundrette across the street?'

Xiang sipped her tea and smiled. 'Of course! I'll take care of things here.'

'If the baby cries, check her diaper and change it if it's wet. Otherwise just hold her for a bit and she'll stop.'

Xiang patted the giant sack of laundry on my shoulder and told me not to worry.

As it was a weekday afternoon, the laundrette was mostly empty. There was just one other woman, a grandmother, who had also come to wash rugs and bedding, like me. She sat in front of the machine and stared vacantly at the fabric spinning around. After I'd put the laundry into the machines, inserted some coins, and started them up, I went to a Sainsbury's a few blocks down to get groceries. By the time I'd bought some things for dinner and returned to the laundrette, the clothes were nearly done. It took another hour or so to dry everything, and then I left.

When I stepped into the alley that led to our building, a strange, sinking feeling came over me. The alley was empty, and all the houses on either side looked deserted. With the laundry sack on one shoulder and the grocery bag in my other hand, I started to walk faster. When I set down the bag and inserted the key into the lock, my hand was shaking. The moment I opened the door, I shouted and clapped my hand over my mouth. Hurriyah Suni lay at the bottom of the stairs like a crumpled-up rag doll. I rushed to pick her up.

'Suni-*ya*! Suni-*ya*!'

Her head fell backward. I screamed and screamed, but the building must have been empty because no one came.

Even after taking her to the hospital and confirming that she was already dead, I couldn't believe it. Grandfather Abdul showed up and tried to lead me away by the arm, but I sat there and refused to move. I couldn't even cry.

'Little Mother,' Grandfather Abdul said, shaking me by the shoulder, 'don't you know? Hurriyah's spirit isn't here. She'll be waiting for you at home.'

Only then did I lean my head into his chest and cry.

When I got home, the flat was a mess. Xiang had ransacked it the moment I left. The bottom drawer of my wardrobe was sticking out — she'd found our emergency stash. After Xiang rushed out, leaving the front door open behind her, Hurriyah must have cried and cried and then tried to make her way to Grandfather Abdul's flat, where she played everyday, by crawling up to the second floor.

I had thought at first that I'd finally found Ali in my dreams, but later I realised the opposite was true. Ali had found me in order to warn me of something. Now I understood the look of pain on his face.

After coming home from burying my daughter, I didn't leave the flat for two weeks.

I'd wanted to have her cremated, but Grandfather Abdul objected cautiously, saying that as Hurriyah was a daughter of Islam, her body shouldn't be destroyed. She was buried in a Muslim cemetery tended by the mosque.

I locked myself in my room and did not go to work. Hurriyah Suni's tiny clothes and toys covered my dresser and shelves. I picked up a rubber baby doll and pressed its belly button. *I love you, Mummy. I love you, Mummy …* The doll muttered the words over and over, then cut off. I hugged it to my chest and collapsed on the floor in tears. After a while, I gathered up all her clothes, sweeping them into the canvas sack I'd used for laundry. I took the sack into the yard, held a match to a bundle of newspaper, and set fire to it. When the flames caught and the clothes started to change colour and shrink as they turned to ash, I bent over and collapsed on the ground again. I covered my mouth, but the words burst out of their own accord.

'Xiang, you hateful woman! I'll kill you!'

Later I understood that all Xiang had really done was remind me of something I'd kept locked inside of me all that time: the bitterness I felt toward every hardship I'd suffered over the course of my long journey.

For the first few days, Luna came by and tried to cheer me up with funny stories, but I had nothing to say in response. I refused all food but water, and would lie in bed all day or sit in a chair by the window and stare out into space. Grandfather Abdul came downstairs now and then with plates of food, but I lay on my side staring at the wall and wouldn't move. He must have been frustrated with me, because one day he took a look at the plate he'd set out the day before, now crusted with untouched food, and confronted me.

'Everyone dies,' he said. 'It doesn't matter whether we die of an accident or illness or by our own hand. Death is not the end. This is a new beginning for Hurriyah. You have to wait until your time comes too, and you can see her again.'

I finally responded: 'Why does God keep making me suffer? I never did anything wrong. What difference does believing and having faith make?'

'God watches over us, but doesn't interfere in our lives. He has no colour, no shape, never laughs or cries, neither sleeps nor forgets, has no beginning and no end, but is always there. Pain and suffering are the results of things we've already done wrong. The purpose of life's good and bad is to teach us to be better people, which is why you have to overcome this and appreciate the beauty of life. That's what God wants from us. So hurry up and eat something and get your strength back!'

'Just leave me be!'

Grandfather Abdul picked up the plate and turned to leave. At the bedroom door, he paused and added: 'When my wife and daughters were shot and I fled Jammu and Kashmir, I was angry at God, too. I didn't understand how He could make good people suffer. But the truth is that all of us who are flesh are already in Hell, on Earth. Anger is a Hell of your own making. God waits silently for us to free ourselves and get closer to Him.'

He closed the door quietly and left. I was so exhausted that I just lay on the bed and wept.

TWELVE

The ceiling opens, and I float up into the dark. As always, a white path appears. I glide over the path to where Chilsung is waiting for me, his tail wagging. I drop toward him, as if I'm collapsing, and try to put my arms around him. But he backs away just a tiny bit and keeps wagging his tail, always keeping the same distance between us.

I'm too sad to live, I say. *Please cheer me up.*

It's okay, Bari. You'll pull through.

Chilsung leads the way. I glide behind him along the white path. We stop at a beach covered in white sand, with large boulders here and there. Grandmother is dressed in white and stands with her back to the sea. The hem of her skirt flutters in the breeze.

Grandma, first I lost my family, and now my husband and daughter are gone.

Consider the world, she says, as I burst into tears. *The people who brush past you on the street are gone as soon as that moment passes. Think of those you saw yesterday, or even a moment ago. They're gone. You can't hear them or see them. Your daughter Suni is here with us.*

Grandmother gestures behind me, and I turn. There she is. She stands next to Chilsung in a white, doll-sized Korean blouse and skirt that match my grandmother's. I put my arms out to pick her up, but just like Chilsung, she takes a step back with each step I move forward. I struggle to reach her, but she keeps her distance.

Don't bother, Grandmother says. *Your body that you treasure so much in life is not you. It houses your spirit. When you leave your body behind, you'll become like us. Sadness, happiness — that all belongs to the world of the living.*

Then I'll join you now.

No, you still have work to do. You've met a lot of people on your travels with questions they need answered.

Yes, and in the old tales, Princess Bari told them she would find the answers during her journey to the otherworld.

Yes, yes, that's right. And you have to find the life-giving water.

Grandmother turns toward the sea. An old, wooden Korean ship with two yellow sails appears. The ship is five, maybe ten times my height. An arched ramp comes down so Chilsung and I can board. Grandmother gives me a little push.

Get on!

As usual, Chilsung goes first and I follow. When I look back, the coastline has disappeared and the ship is floating in the middle of the blackness. We sail through the sky instead of on water. Chilsung and I stand on the ship's bridge, under the canopy.

First we'll cross a sea of fire, Chilsung explains. *Then a sea of blood. Finally, after we pass the sea of sand that swallows even the lightest goose down, we'll reach the iron castle.*

Where is that?

At the end of the western sky.

We leave the darkness, and the blazing sea of fire begins. Flames shoot into the air on either side of the ship, and acrid clouds of dark smoke billow around us. I cannot make out any shapes in the fire below, only sounds. I hear the thunder of bombs exploding, guns firing, bullets whizzing, airplanes and helicopters and tanks and armoured cars flying, racing, and rolling by amid constant gunfire and explosions. A crowd lets out a tremendous roar. Women and children scream. Voices shout.

March!

Hands up! Don't move!

Exterminate the devils!

Glory to God!

Shoot them all! Kill them! Smash them! Wipe them all out!

The din threatens to make my head explode, no matter how hard I press my hands over my ears.

Then the flames and smoke vanish, and darkness surrounds the ship again. The noise fades and finally stops. I lower my hands.

Oh, that was awful, Chilsung says. *That hell was built in your world first. That's why it looks the same in this world.*

The sky slowly fills with a reddish glow as in the late evening, and down below I can see waves of dark red: the ship is crossing the sea of blood. I begin to make out shadowy buildings far off in the distance, like a city skyline.

What city is that? I ask Chilsung.

Those are the ships of the dead. They stay here in the sea of blood.

As we get closer, I see grey ships of different shapes bobbing this way and that. Standing on the decks in the dim lamplight are men, women, and children, naked or dressed in rags. Among them, I recognise the people I met on the road and in mountain villages between Musan and Puryong. Thinking I might see my sister Hyun or the rest of my family, I search the crowd.

Finally, I spot them. There's my mother and Jung and Sook, who were sent to Puryong. Hyun, who froze to death in the mountains, is with them. Ah, so they all died after all. Just as I can always tell when I'm dreaming, I know that this place is not the world of the living but a vision of the otherworld. I call out to them.

Mother! Sisters! Hyun!

But all they do is stand in a row and face front, as if they cannot hear me.

The scene changes without mercy, showing me every corner of the inside of the ship in turn. People of all races are on board. It carries souls from every corner of the world who were starved, tortured, worked or beaten to death, or who were terminally ill, bombed, burned, drowned, or who died of a broken heart.

Someone leans over the front of the ship and shouts: *Tell us the reason for our suffering! Why are we here?*

It's Becky.

I don't understand this, I call to her. *Why are you all in the same boat?*

This is the inside of your mind. Don't forget my question.

As the ship she is in slides past mine, I shout: *I'll give you an answer when I return!*

Another ship passes slowly. Glowing red torches light every inch from stern to bow. Standing in rows inside it are people wielding spears, arrows, knives, and guns, people with their hair dishevelled, their arms torn off, legs severed, heads missing, people dressed in blood-soaked uniforms, wrapped in gauze, leaning on crutches, eyes bandaged, people struggling to escape.

I see Lady Emily's father and grandfather. I see American and British soldiers, and I see my husband's younger brother Usman with a long beard and a round, white *topi* prayer hat on his head. He calls out: *Bari, tell us why evil wins! And why we are stuck here with our enemies!*

I shout: *I'll tell you when I return!*

The ship I am in slowly glides over the surface of the sea of blood. Another ship approaches. It is jet-black from sails to hull. Inside this ship, men and women stand, their mouths shut tight, chests and stomachs hung with clusters of explosives. Some of the men are stripped naked, their bodies twisted and deformed by burns and shrapnel, while others have no bodily form at all and instead their flesh — which had been blown apart and scattered in every possible direction — hovers in the air like a swarm of flies forming the vague shape of a person.

Old and young men with long beards and stubborn faces. Women with *hijabs* and haggard faces, or with distorted faces that look like they've been burned, bodies covered in bruises and open wounds from the lashings they received. Women covered from head to toe in loose, shapeless *burqas*.

I see an unfamiliar man with grenades strapped to his chest shaking his fist at me.

He yells: *Tell us the meaning of our deaths!*

A *burqa*-clad woman standing next to him murmurs behind the fabric covering her face: *Tell me what my death means, too.*

Unsure of what their questions even mean, I reply: *I'll tell you when I return.*

Another ship approaches. It seems to have no torches or lamps, nor even a single passenger on deck. It drifts toward us as silent as death, without even the slightest sign of movement on board. Then, in the darkness, I begin to make out faint shapes.

The silence is broken by a spooky laugh. The government officials who took my father away are there, as are the men who chased us from our home and the men who tormented and sold my sister Mi after she crossed the Tumen River alone. The loan sharks in Dalian, the men I saw on the smuggling ship: they are all on board. The snakeheads who shoved us into the containers, the men who raped us in the dark belly of the ship, even the fat brothel owner who laughed when she saw my flat chest: they are there too.

Ah, and the worst of them all: terrifying, hateful Xiang twists up her face and glares at me. As the ships we are in slide past each other, she shouts: *This boat carries the people you hate most. When will we be set free?*

I tear at my chest and yell back: *I will* never *set you free! When will* we *be free of* you?

I shudder and say automatically: *I'll tell you when I return.*

The ship crosses the sea of blood, and is enveloped in darkness again. The sky grows light. Fine sand floats in midair like fog. Below the ship stretches a wilderness of sand with no end in sight, no matter how far I look. There is nothing but sand all the way to the faint horizon.

This is the sea of sand that swallows even the lightest goose down, Chilsung explains.

What kind of place is this?

Just what it sounds like. It swallows up everything.

I look out over the clean, peaceful-looking white sand. Something is moving. People, each in different attire, hold sacred texts aloft. They talk loudly in languages the others cannot understand, barely able to keep their footing in the sand. There are more: religious leaders from every corner of the world are assembled there. From their wigs to their hats and their gowns and their black and their white, they all look the same. They speak different languages, each saying different things, which makes their words sound like some kind of peculiar incantation.

They are so intent on drowning each other out that their words become garbled and lose all meaning. Their faces flush dark red, their eyes bulge, and they raise their sacred texts with one hand while waving the other at the ground and at the sky. But there is no chance that the sand will simply leave them be — they struggle to keep their balance as their legs slowly sink into it. They sink to their waists, their chests, their throats, and then their heads disappear and all I can see are their flailing arms before they vanish without a trace, and there is nothing left but sand. All is quiet for a moment, but suddenly the sand spits them back out; their bodies fly up, and they resume their endless talking and arguing. Then the sand slowly sucks them under again. Over this monotonous, noisy, ludicrous sea of sand that swallows even the lightest goose down, our ship drifts silently.

The ship arrives at a beach that looks similar to the one from which we departed. The sand bristles with rocks, and dark stone mountains tower in the distance. Standing firmly at the top of one of the mountains is a cast-iron castle, rusted to a reddish-black. Each square window in the perfectly square castle glows with light.

You have to go in there and bring back the spirit flower and the life-giving water, Chilsung says. But I cannot bring myself to leave the ship.

I'm scared, I tell him. *I can't do this on my own.*

The story that's been handed down to us from long, long ago says that Bari is the only one who can do this.

No sooner do I set my foot on the gangplank than I am already standing on land. Chilsung holds a wrapped bundle in his teeth; he tosses it over the side of the ship. When I open it, a copper rattle, a copper mirror, and *gaetteok* made from sorghum flour are inside.

Those are from your grandmother, Chilsung says. *You'll need them where you're going. Call me when you're done, and I'll bring the boat back.*

I sling the bundle over my shoulder and start climbing the rugged mountain slope. Rocks tumble past; when I grab for a handhold, the rocks crumble or break away. I get stuck in a ravine and have to shimmy my way out and resume my climb. My palms, elbows, and knees are all scraped, skinned, and bleeding. When I finally reach a spot where I can see the castle gate, the path ends abruptly at the edge of a deep, dark cliff. I hear someone laughing on a rock right next to me.

Kar-kar-kar! Where you think you're goin', Stupidhead? Karr-rr-rr!

I look up to see the magpie sitting there. I'm too happy to see a familiar face to get angry.

I have to go in there and get the spirit flower and the life-giving water. Help me!

The magpie flicks his tail a few times, then flaps his wings and lands lightly on my shoulder.

How 'bout that rattle, hey? How 'bout that rattle?

I open the bundle and pull out the rattle. I hold it overhead and give it a good shake. A stone bridge appears in the dark. The magpie and I cross. With each step, the bridge collapses behind us and vanishes.

The castle gate is shut tight, and is guarded by a pair of hairy sentinels, each with a single horn protruding from its head. They wear armour with dragons on the front, and wield fiery clubs.

Egh! Too scary! The magpie warbles on my shoulder. *One cake each! Throw it, throw it!*

The guards open their red eyes wide and shout: *Who goes there?*

I throw a *gaetteok* into each of their gaping mouths. They swallow them and instantly bow to me. The castle gate screeches open. I hurry inside.

I cross a long stone path and come to a smaller gate. A pair of dogs with fire blazing inside their mouths stand guard on stone slabs on either side of the gate. They jump down, growl, and bare their teeth.

One each, one each.

Even before the magpie can finish muttering the words, I toss more *gaetteok*. The dogs swallow them and return meekly to their stone slabs.

Inside the gate is a wide plaza where countless guards — hundreds upon hundreds, if not more — are lined up for a parade inspection. I see several paths at the far end of the plaza.

White path, white path, the magpie chitters.

I grab two fistfuls of *gaetteok* so I can throw them at a moment's notice, and I make a run for the white path in the middle. The guards break formation and rush at me from both sides. I throw the *gaetteok* in all directions. The plaza descends into a mêlée as they tackle each other and fall over themselves to grab the food.

I make it out of the plaza and reach a big, tree-lined garden. In the middle, red, blue, yellow, and white flowers are in full, glorious bloom.

Spirit flower! Spirit flower! the magpie cackles.

I pace back and forth, unsure of which among the hundreds of flowers to pick.

Stupidhead! Only the spirit flower. Only the spirit flower.

The magpie can't tell me anything more. I think about the white path and select the white flowers. I don't take many — just three.

Kar-kar-kar! Well done, Stupidhead! Karr-rr-rr!

I tuck the three flowers inside my shirt. Buoyed by the bird's laughing praise, I hop and dance about joyfully, straight over to where the garden ends.

A fiery pond blocks the next part of the castle. This

time I take out the rattle without asking the magpie first, and raise it overhead. The stone bridge reappears above the pond. I run across, the bridge collapsing noisily behind me with each step.

As soon as I am inside, everything goes black; all around me are voices screaming and crying. Even the magpie seems frightened. His voice is low and trembles like a baby frog.

This is it. The end of the western sky. The hell of eighty-four thousand, eighty-four thousand sufferings.

The ceiling of the castle seems to reach as far up as the sky itself, and the air is filled with fog or smoke. When I look around, I see that the walls are filled with cells from floor to ceiling, like a beehive. I hear voices ordering others, spurring others, and more voices responding; the sounds of beating, and the sounds of weeping and wailing. I feel as if I am standing in deep jungle surrounded by howling creatures. My heart pounds, I am dizzy and I think I might collapse. Without help from the magpie, I reach into my shirt and pull out a spirit flower. I toss it into the air as forcefully as I can. It soars up, then coasts down slowly on a stray breeze. The flower pops like a balloon and tens of thousands of petals scatter in all directions, drifting about like snowflakes before turning into bright, white light. Words begin to flow through me, in time with the beat of an unseen drum.

Gather, souls! Gather 'round, spirits!
Here, beneath the western sky,
out here, at the ends of the Earth,
those who sinned,
those who were sinned against,

souls bound together in Hell,
caught in the endless cycle
of life, death, rebirth, death, life.
Unfetter yourself, unfetter each other,
and rise up through the nine heavens.
Return to life! Return!

The air slowly fills with light, and the iron castle begins to crumble. Chunks of rock and metal melt away the moment the light touches them like ice in the sun. Soon there is nothing but flat land. The freed spirits crowd together: sinners who have lost their eyes, sinners without arms, sinners without legs, sinners without heads, sinners who have lost the entire lower halves of their bodies. They come pouring out, and even the guards cast down their weapons, rush forward and dance. The land is filled with dancing spirits.

I turn around. There is the third and final part of the castle. I walk toward the heavy gate, which creaks open slowly by itself. A cold wind comes whooshing out. The magpie flies off my shoulder.

Egh! Too scary! I can't go. You go alone. You go.

I step inside. There's another wide plaza. At the centre is a big, black, foul-smelling pond. A half-moon-shaped bridge arcs over its centre. I start to cross the bridge, but an enormous cast-iron dragon suddenly appears on the other side. It rushes at me, clinking and clanging, its jaws open wide, spewing fireballs. The flames touch the surface of the pond, and in a flash the whole thing is ablaze. Flowers of fire flicker and flare up all around.

I pull the final item from the bundle: the copper mirror. I hold it out in front of me, and as the light reflects off it, the flames freeze in place. The fire comes to a stop, like snowflakes on the branches of trees in winter or frost blooming across a windowpane. The iron dragon begins to crack; it breaks into pieces that fall to the floor and shatter, then turn to powder, then blow away. I cross the plaza and climb a staircase. At the top, I enter a high-ceilinged room. The King of Hell, in his shining golden armour and helmet with the visor down over his face, stands there waiting for me, his fiery curved sword held aloft.

He booms: *I don't have a physical form, but I took this one for you!*

I'm here to free you too, I tell him, *so behave yourself.*

He swings his sword. The flame wraps around my body like a whip and flings me away, hard. I hit the wall and fall to the ground. I am barely able to pull myself up, but I take a step toward him and the flame wraps around me again and hurls me across the room. As I stand, I hold up the copper mirror and shine it on the King of Hell. The light bounces off it, and his golden armour turns to jelly and slides off him, revealing the tiny body of an old man, bent over and frail with age, clad in rags. He sinks to the floor.

Oh … I'm so tired! he mutters, in a voice no bigger than a mosquito's. I press him for answers to my questions.

There must be some knowledge I can take back with me.

Now all mysteries will be solved.

Where is the life-giving water?

The old man tilts his head back as if lacking even the strength to lift his arms.

Is there such a thing? There is a small spring out there, but that's just the regular water we use to cook rice.

I turn and exit through a back door. At the bottom of the stairs is a garden with a small well. I hurry down, crouch next to the well, and scoop up water in my cupped hands. I drink from it twice. It tastes sweet and refreshing, just like the spring water from the mountains and rivers of my hometown. Nothing more. Disappointed, I stand up. Then I remember the flowers in my shirt, so I take one out and toss it into the air. It explodes, and as the petals drift down and turn to light, the final part of the castle is engulfed in an enormous cloud of dust and begins to collapse.

Everything vanishes, and just as before, there is only a tranquil field with a few rocks and the quietly settling air. The magpie has returned and is perched on a rock, flicking his tail around and preening his feathers with his beak.

There's no such thing as 'life-giving water', I say bitterly.

The magpie shrieks with laughter. *Karr-rr-rr! Stupidhead! It's what you drank, what you drank.*

I look around hurriedly at the empty field.

The magpie chatters again: *No one can take it, not the life-giving water.* The bird keeps laughing — *karr-rr-rr karr-rr-rr* — and flies away.

I plod toward the beach. When I reach the spot where the water rushes up onto the sand, I call out inside my head: *Chilsung-ah! Chilsung-ah!*

The ship appears, and the gangplank descends. The moment my foot touches the first step, I am aboard, and Chilsung is welcoming me with his wagging tail.

We go up into the crow's nest, and the ship starts to float away.

I didn't get the life-giving water, I say weakly.

Chilsung swishes his tail but doesn't reply. The ship glides over the sea of sand. The variously attired men are still flailing their arms and shouting and sinking into the sand and re-emerging. As I look down at them, I mutter: *Either take turns and let each other talk, or work together and speak for each other. Or maybe just don't say anything at all.*

The sea of sand vanishes. Now it's just normal blue sky and blue ocean with fat clouds overhead.

We cross the sea of blood again. I see the ships floating like black spots in the red sky. The grey ship approaches, carrying people of all shapes and colours, refugees in tattered rags, my mother and sisters, souls from all over the world who were starved, tortured, worked or beaten to death, bombed, burned, drowned, terminally ill or died of a broken heart. Just as before, Becky leans her body over the front of the ship and looks at me.

Tell us why we had to suffer like this. Why are we here?

Something seems to take over my tongue. My voice turns young and high-pitched as someone else speaks through me.

They say we're here because of desire. In our desire to live better than others, we are cruel to each other. That's why the god who rides that boat with you says he has also suffered. By forgiving them, you help him.

When the words stop, the scene ends. The grey ship disappears without a trace. The red ship lit with torches approaches, carrying the people wielding weapons, people with their hair loose and dishevelled, arms torn off, legs severed, heads missing, people in blood-soaked uniforms, wrapped in gauze, leaning on crutches, eyes bandaged, people struggling to escape. This ship, which carries Lady Emily's father and grandfather and my husband's younger brother Usman, draws close.

Usman calls out to me again: *Did you find out why evil wins, and why we are stuck here with our enemies?*

I babble in the tiny voice of a little girl: *There are no winners in war. What the living call justice is always one-sided.*

The scene ends. The red ship vanishes.

The third ship, which has been waiting at a distance, approaches, jet-black from sails to hull and carrying men with explosives strapped to their bodies, men whose flesh and bones have been blown apart and are barely maintaining the outline of a body, like a swarm of dayflies hovering in the air. Fathers, brothers, and husbands who took it upon themselves to punish their daughters, sisters, and wives all ride the ship together. The man with the grenades dangling from his chest shakes his fist at me.

Tell us the meaning of our deaths!

The little-girl voice bursts out of me again: *The gods grieve for the hopelessness you feel. They cannot help you with your despair.*

The woman in the *burqa* murmurs through the fabric covering her face: *And what about the meaning of my death?*

I look at these phantoms, and for the first time I cry as if my heart is breaking.

Men covered you up. Then outsiders said you had to take off your veils in order to be free, while your own men said you had to keep them on in order to maintain control at home. Your faces are the ones the gods grieve for the most.

The black ship vanishes like a soap bubble bursting. The last ship floats toward me, silent as death, without the slightest sign of movement on deck, as if there are no torches, no light, nor even a single passenger. Then the silence is broken by whispers of laughter, and I can see the officials who tore my family apart on board, along with the men who betrayed my sister Mi, the loan sharks of Dalian, the snakeheads, the brothel owner.

And Xiang. She leans over the side, pushing her skinny face with its protruding cheekbones toward me as she shouts: *Everyone you hate the most is here. When will we be set free?*

The child's voice comes out of me again: *Mama is the one who's bound. When she is free of her hatred, you too will be free.*

The ship slips past and slowly recedes. I sob in the little-girl voice: *Poor Mama … Poor Mama …*

At last, I realise that Hurriyah Suni has been inside of me, sailing with me the whole time. The black ship vanishes into the dark.

The old Korean boat I am on crosses the sea of blood. I pull the final spirit flower from my heavy, aching chest and toss it into the air. It hisses like the fuse on a firecracker and explodes, sending thousands, tens of thousands of petals through the air. They turn into bright light and illuminate sky and sea. Countless souls rise out of the water and turn into specks of light. They float up into the sky and unite. The sea of blood becomes a blue ocean, and instantly, the blue stretches all the way out to where the sea of fire begins.

For the nearly fifteen days that I spent locked in my room, barely moving, time seemed to stand still. After one long continuous dream, I had other choppy, disconnected dreams. Their plots all intertwined. I remembered the visions and scenes from those dreams in such a way that I could have described them to anyone later with perfect consistency.

I sipped water and occasionally ate soup that Luna made for me — it was a more intense fast than at Ramadan. Grandfather Abdul had stopped by several times to check on me initially, but he must have decided that I needed some space. Every now and then, I heard his footsteps on the stairs. They would grow softer the closer he got to my door, but then after a brief pause I would hear him tiptoe away again.

One morning, I got up and took a warm bath and then prepared breakfast. I took the food upstairs to Grandfather Abdul's flat, and we ate our first hearty breakfast together in a long time. He smiled at me and watched my every move, but didn't say anything until we were sipping tea afterward.

'I know it took some time, but I can't tell you how good it is to see that you've finally sent Hurriyah to God. Thank you for getting through it.'

'I think she's still with me.'

Grandfather Abdul was quiet for a moment, then nodded.

'If that's what you want to believe,' he said. 'But at some point you'll have to let her go. All souls begin new lives after death.'

'Grandfather, how wonderful would it be if there were a water of life that could save the world? If only I could find it …'

He looked at me, his gaze soft, and waited for me to continue.

'I had this long, long dream that went on for several days. A dream in which I was searching for a life-giving water.'

He took my hand gently and stroked it.

'I don't know what this life-giving water is that you were hoping for, but we have to weep for each other in order to save ourselves. No matter what awful things we go through, we cannot abandon hope in the world or in others.'

I went back to work at Tongking. Everyone was happy to see me. Around the same time, I got a phone call from Uncle Lou. He said he was sorry to be the one to tell me the news.

'Xiang jumped out of a window. She must've been on something.'

After his call, I went into the break room and sat by myself. One of the scenes from the dream came back faintly. I pictured Xiang asking me when I would set her free. I sat there quietly with my face directed at the ceiling, until the tears rolled off my chin. I wasn't crying from sadness, but from shame. A truly unbearable surge of regret washed over me. I'd been so exhausted with looking after myself that I'd never once gone to see her or even thought of trying to help her. And I'd hated her so much for Suni's death.

—

The following spring, a new war began, in Iraq. On top of that, news reporters kept saying that war would soon break out in Korea as well. One day, I happened to see a television documentary about the famine I'd experienced long ago in the North. There were scenes of war and other terrible images, but of course not a word was said about the countless souls and spirits I'd met on my journey. Everyone gaped at the television screen like they were watching a fireworks display. And they ate and they drank and they talked and talked.

I hadn't been to see Lady Emily in ages, and she hadn't requested any house calls from me in some time. I finally did go to see her, because of some news I'd received from Leeds. Grandfather Abdul had gotten a call from Ali's father. He said a government official had come to their house asking about Ali and Usman, and wanted to know when they'd left for Pakistan, where they were headed, whether there had been any contact from Usman afterward, and whether or not it was certain that Ali had gone there in search of his brother. Before the official left their house, he'd told Ali's father: *Your son is alive, but not free.*

'I knew it all along!' I had shouted at Grandfather Abdul. 'I knew he was still alive!' I'd felt strongly from the beginning that he was alive somewhere, and in pain.

Lady Emily's life had changed completely since she'd started raising her deceased husband's child. The house was nothing like what it used to be: all the curtains were open wide, and every vase and flowerpot was brimming with succulent green leaves and blossoms. Even the staircase, which had always been dark before, now had sunlight streaming down on it from the windows. I heard the baby fussing and crawling around. Lady Emily greeted me in the parlour downstairs. She was wearing a brightly coloured dress, and had even done her makeup.

'Bari, how have you been? I almost didn't get to see you. We're moving out to the country soon. This house will be empty for a while.'

She filled me in on everything that had happened since I had last seen her. 'I went to see Anthony's mother in jail. I also set her up with a lawyer.'

I told her calmly about the things that had happened to me as well. Her eyes reddened, and she held my hand and said, 'Oh no!' and 'you poor thing' as she comforted me. I told her the latest news about Ali, and even before I could ask for her help, she said: 'I'll find out where he is. There's not much else I can do, but I can at least do that.'

I stood up and bowed to her. 'That's why I came. I just … want to know where he is.'

After that, things were quiet for a while. Then Auntie Sarah came to find me at Tongking. She took me out to a café.

'Lady Emily has left for the countryside, so she asked me to come see you.' Then she grew quiet. I suppressed my impatience and waited. 'She said your husband is currently being held in detention in another country. They have no idea when he'll be released. And now the war has started up again … Bari, are you okay?'

I nodded and showed her a smile. Now that I had confirmation Ali was alive, I couldn't ask for anything more.

The year I turned twenty-one, Ali returned — like a

sudden rain shower at the end of a long drought. He was released to his parents in Leeds sometime in March, then came to London carrying a single, small backpack as if he'd only been gone a few days. I went to meet him at the train station. Though I saw my tall man's head sticking out above the crowd of people pouring off the platform, I didn't run to him. I stood and waited instead, my heart pounding. He was walking with his father and almost walked right by without seeing me, but I reached out and tapped him on the arm.

'You're back,' I said.

He hung back for a moment and then grabbed me in his arms. We stood there holding each other as people brushed past. That day, he told his family that Usman really was dead.

His father stared up at the ceiling. 'He was just a child,' he lamented.

Grandfather Abdul said: 'We are all just children.' He lowered his head and said a brief prayer. When he was done, he said: 'This war is a hell caused by the arrogance of the powerful and the desperation of the poor. We are poor and have nothing to give, but we must have faith that we can still help others. This is the only way the world will ever get any better. The Lord said: "Beware the flames of anger. They harm only the least fortunate."'

Ali was less talkative than before, but in exchange he'd become a warmer, gentler man. We used our words sparingly, as if we'd agreed not to talk about the ordeals we'd gone through. He made a few brief comments about the dark, sweltering prison cell he'd been kept in and the deep scars on his wrists from the restraints, and I spoke in fragments about carrying and giving birth to Hurriyah Suni and my short time with her. Each time our eyes met, he smiled, cradled my face with one of his giant pot-lid-sized hands, and gazed long and hard at me.

After my husband came home, I became pregnant again. He quit his job driving cabs, with its unpredictable pay and mandatory night shifts. We opened a cute little shop that sold sandwiches and kebabs near Camden Market. In the mornings, I helped Ali out and manned the register, and in the afternoons I went to work at Tongking as usual. In the evenings, we ate dinner with Grandfather Abdul. Our lives were so peaceful that we nearly started to believe the world had changed.

One day, Ali and I had left the house in the morning and were riding the bus to Camden. We crossed Waterloo Bridge and were going up the street toward Southampton Row when we heard a deafening explosion. The cars all stopped, and people started running. We got off the bus and crossed the street. Smoke and flames were rising from the direction of Russell Square, and we followed other people there to see what had happened. A bus had exploded in the middle of the road. People said there had been a second blast at King's Cross Station. The top of a double-decker had blown off, and the lower half was demolished. Sheets of twisted metal, bus seats, and broken glass were strewn all over the street, and the windows in nearby shops had shattered. Bodies lay sprawled on the ground, and there was blood everywhere. Injured people staggered to their feet; others walked around dazed and bleeding. I leaned against Ali, feeling as if I might collapse, and turned my face away. He wrapped his arm around me and we left. The street filled with the sound of police and ambulance sirens.

'Baby, I'm sorry,' I murmured, my hands around my swollen belly, breathing hard as we hurried away.

Ali and I made our way between the stopped cars sitting bumper-to-bumper. With both hands, I wiped tears that wouldn't stop coming, and turned to look back: Ali was crying too.